The Hip-Hop Series

Word Works by, for and in the Language of the
New Urban Generation

Www.PenknifePress.Com

Emotional

Drippings

Emotional Drippings
Stories of Love, Lust and Addiction
by
Tony Lindsay

Penknife Press   Chicago, Illinois

Copyright © 2013 by Tony Lindsay
All rights reserved under International and Pan-American Copyright Conventions.
Published in the United States of America by Penknife Press, Ltd., Chicago, Illinois.

ISBN 978-1-59997-018-9

Library of Congress Control Number: 2013936430

Manufactured in the United States of America

Section One Lust

Section Two Love

Section Three Addiction

Tony Lindsay

Visiting My Man

It was never supposed to be me riding on this dirty old school bus, especially not me as a grownup. When I was a kid, I rode this bus with my mama. We rode downstate to see her man, and I didn't like it then.

Well, to be truthful when I was a kid I did like going on the long ride and playing around with the other kids. We always made up fun games on the long ride, like find the green and blue cars - or the brown and red ones. I remember it was hard to find cars with a combination of colors. Oh, and the lunches, I almost forgot about the surprise snacks the women on the bus would bring: cakes, rolls, candy, pies, "something sweet for the trip," they would say.

Since I have been catching this bus as a grown person, none of the adults have brought something sweet for the trip. Maybe next week I'll bring the kids something. Another fun thing about the bus ride was we got to hear grown folks' business. The bus was small, so we heard everything. We knew who was getting out of prison soon, and who was really guilty, and who was helping who sneak what in, and who was going to go to jail next if they wasn't careful. We acted like we weren't listening, but we were. At least the girls were. I don't think any of the boys listened. If they had, I doubt that four out of the five boys that rode the bus with us would be locked up now. The bus rides stopped being fun after the second year. Once I found what people that didn't ride the bus said about those of us who did. "Jailhouse wives and they kids," is what we were called. Or they called us, "State property kids." I hated the names. I was already being called, skinny, nappy headed, and buck-toothed. I didn't need any more teasing tags.

It seemed like everybody in the neighborhood knew that the dirty

Emotional Drippings

old school bus parked in Mt. Zion's parking lot every Saturday morning was going to the prison. Over forty years ago some of the jail house wives in the neighborhood got together and hired the bus for the ride downstate. When a couple of them died, they left money to keep the trip going for the families of inmates. It doesn't cost a dime for us to ride downstate to visit, just a little pride.

When I began to whine to my mother about being teased, she stopped making me go with her. The man she was visiting wasn't my daddy anyway, so it really didn't make any sense for me to go through the embarrassment. I told myself that was an embarrassment that I would not have to go through again, never. Obviously I was wrong.

When Kenny first got sent downstate, I had enough money to rent a car and a driver to take me to see my man. Five years and three lawyers later, I am on the dirty old school bus with the other "jailhouse wives". We, my husband and me, ain't broke, but I can't afford to spend money foolishly. The pride of my childhood gives in to the budgeting of an adult wife with a husband in prison.

I'm not as embarrassed as I was when I was a kid, but it still bothers me a little to walk around the corner to the bus. I live in the same neighborhood I grew up in, two blocks from my mama and Big Mama's house. So everybody knows where I'm strolling to on Saturday mornings.

When my husband comes home, we will live well. I wasn't stupid with his money. We got a couple of buildings, and I went in with my brother and brought a barbeque-rib joint and a Laundromat. We ain't gonna be ballin' anymore, but we gonna live pretty good.

Kenny is proud of how I worked his money. I thought he was gonna be mad when I told him I sold his trucks and his Lexus. But I can't drive, and them boys, his ex-friends, were offering so much money for them that I had to sell them. With that money, plus with using a little of the money he left under the bathroom floor, I was able to buy our first building and pay for those useless lawyers. Well, I shouldn't call the lawyers useless; they did get him a reduced sentence. He will be home for good in two years. The last lawyer is the one that got us the conjugal visits. With Kenny being a model prisoner, he said it wasn't a problem.

Natalie, the older woman in the seat in front of me has been having conjugal visits with her husband for eleven years. This is my first one, and I have been sort of the joke of the bus ride because of it. I been smiling and nodding my head with them, but contrary to what they think, this sister ain't hard up or desperately in need of some beef. I am well taken care of in that department. Matter of fact, I am doing better than I was when Kenny was out. Kenny's and my thing was never based on sex, at least not for me.

My high school flame and me started kickin' it after the first year Kenny got sent downstate. I am a young twenty three year old woman with real needs that likes male company. My high-school flame is married and in love with his wife. So it ain't **gonna** be no drama when Kenny gets out. He'll have his wife and I'll have my husband. We both know what we doing is only temporary. At least the frequency we are doing it now is temporary. We won't be able to get away with seeing so much of each other once Kenny comes home.

What I'm worried about though, is what if Kenny can tell I been with another man? My old flame is bigger than Kenny is down there. A lot bigger, he's longer and thicker, and I'm wondering if the tight glove fit Kenny use to brag about is still there. I don't feel any looser

Emotional Drippings

or larger. Every time me and my old flame do it he says I am as tight as I was in high-school. If he goes in too soon or too fast it hurts me just as much as when I was in high school. So things feel the same to me.

He says I won't have anything to worry about with Kenny because my stuff is still real good and tight. But I think it's real good to him because his thing is bigger than Kenny's. When I put on my gloves after my mama puts her big hands in them, I can tell that she's has worn them. I'm afraid Kenny is gonna be able to tell that my flame has been inside me and messed up his glove tight fit. But I really don't feel any larger down there.

This is not the same bus I caught as kid, but ain't much difference in it. A narrow aisle, hard green vinyl seats, a rubber mat covering the aisle floor, and a white metal ceiling. Looks the same, but it's newer. I know every family on this bus. They are all from my neighborhood.

I thought I was gonna have plenty of time before Kenny came home. That my stuff would get back like it was if I stopped doing it with my flame about a month or so before Kenny came home. But shoot, doing it with him has gotten so good to me that I gave him some this morning when he stopped by on his way to work. He makes sex enjoyable for me. Kenny didn't.

My mama said I was being stupid to mess around with my old flame. She claims she was loyal to her husband for the eight years he was in jail, but I know for a fact she wasn't loyal to my daddy when he wasn't locked up. Which is why he left us fifteen years ago, and I seriously doubt that she was loyal to her man of my childhood, despite what she claims.

She forgets that I lived with her during most of those eight years. I saw her going out to the Eastside Club every Wednesday night and not coming home until Thursday afternoon. I know that went on for at least two of the years that he was locked down. My mama thinks everybody in the world is stupid but her. Her getting saved and sanctified may have washed her mind clean of all the wrong stuff she did, but I still remember, and so does Big Mama. We laugh at her selective memory.

I hope what Big Mama told me to do about my down there concern works. She said it worked for her after having nine kids. She told me granddaddy was a happy, sexually satisfied husband until he died. I believe her cause my granddaddy never had a mean word to say to anybody. I can remember him always rubbing and patting Big Mama. Where ever she was, he was always nearby. Big Mama said the alum worked for her mama and my mama too. I asked my mama about the alum, but she acted like she didn't know what I was talking about, and said she never had such concerns.

Big Mama said I should douche with the alum mix about a half hour before Kenny and me get intimate. I used the alum mix this morning after me and my flame did it, and I used the mix right before I got on this bus and my stuff feels real tight now. It feels like it sucking up inside me. I don't know if I'm gonna use anymore before me and Kenny get together, but I brought some just in case. If it worked for Big Mama after nine kids, it should work behind my flame.

I really didn't mean to get started up with my old flame the way that I have. It was just to be once for old times, but the first date lead to a second and a third. The next thing I know we are going at it every other day, and now we have no plans to stop. So I'm laughing with the wives on the bus, but believe me, I am not in need.

Natalie whispers for me not to expect too much from the first time

Emotional Drippings

with Kenny. She says he's going to be so excited that he might not get three good pumps in. She says by the third visit things will get better, and she asks are my conjugal visits overnight. I tell her no, only one hour. She says it wasn't until after his seventh year that her husband got overnights. There is a nice, grown lady, auntie type smile on her face. I feel her pat me on my arm. "Things are going to be fine, baby," she says. Natalie turns back around in her seat and talks to her daughter.

My mind goes back to me and Kenny's actual first time. I was not planning on giving him any because all the neighborhood girls had him and his boys spoiled. It was rumored that Kenny was doing it with some of my girls' mamas, and he was the same age as me. To me, that was just plain nasty.

Kenny and his boys had neighborhood and city baller status because they had been rollin' good in the crack game for about two years. He sat courtside at the games and ringside at the fights. He had flown girls first class to Jamaica where they stayed in fancy hotels and all that. He had four one carat earrings in his ears, two in each, and his pinky ring cost more than Big Mama's house. So when he rolled up on me that cool fall evening in his Lexus, I wasn't try to hear a thing he had to say.

I didn't like ballers because they treated women as if they were disposable. Every girl in the neighborhood was supposed to lie down for them because they were rich. Not me. I wasn't going for it. At least I thought I wasn't.

He didn't roll up me talking that going to Jamaica or that fight and game mess. The first thing he said to me was that he thought I was "wifey" material, and that he was looking to settle down. He said his father had told him I was a good girl and that he should take me to church.

The big baller rolled up on me because his daddy told him to. We went to church for about two months, then to the movies, the theatres, out to dinner, and shopping. I liked shopping the most.

When we did it the first time it wasn't remarkable or anything, at least not to me. He asked me to marry him right after that. I came down a little on my menstrual, and he thought it was virgin blood. I didn't tell him any different because I was getting use to his spending. Besides, he was only the second man I had done it with in my life, and since my high school flame didn't live in the neighborhood no one knew about him, and I was never one to tell my business. So was I head over heels in love with him? No, but we are in love now and that's all that matters.

Everybody on the bus is back into their own conversations and the teasing about my conjugal visit has stopped. I think I may have overdid the alum. My stuff is getting uncomfortable. Good thing the bus is pulling into the gate, I need something inside of me to work against the tightening.

We all get off the bus together, but me, Natalie, and Maxine, the other wife with conjugal visits are escorted to another smaller building. Walking down the sunny concrete path alongside me, Natalie she says we are going to the cottage. What she calls a cottage is a short one story building. We have to stand outside in the cold waiting to get buzzed through the steel double doors.

Once in the cottage, we all are escorted to large community shower room where we are told to strip. This throws me back a little. I haven't had to strip before, but seeing Natalie not hesitating to disrobe, I do the same.

We are given laundry baskets to hold our belongings. The three of

Emotional Drippings

us are standing butt naked behind these little baskets when two female guards walk in. I see Natalie bend over and spread her butt cheeks without a word said, Maxine does the same, and so do I.

One guard is going through our clothes in the basket while the other is behind us with a flash light. I feel fingers open my coochie pie and go up in my bootie hole. I don't like this one bit. The guard behind us walks out without a word said. The others get dressed, and so do I. We don't say a thing to each other. The guard that went through our belongings says we can only wear the clothes we have on to the dorm rooms, our coats are to stay in the baskets.

We follow her out of the showers and down a corridor full of rooms. She points to the first room. It's for me, 16A. I go inside. There is a small twin sized bed and a cassette player on a tiny table next to the bed. On the far white wall is blue-face clock. It reads ten fifty five. Inside the cassette player is 'A Soul Lovers' tape with songs by Luther, the Temptations, Marvin Gaye, Mary J. Blige, and others. The twin bed is covered with a thin brown blanket. I pull it back to see a cover sheet and a fitted sheet. I sit on the bed and wait.

Outside in the hall, I hear one of the female guards arguing in a whisper, but I don't hear a response from the one she's arguing with. Something is said about her doing her part and why should she have to act as if it was okay. I hear the guard's rapid steps past the door and in walks Kenny, and damn, he looks good to me.

He says something about it being good to see me. I ain't hearing him really because my man has swollen up with muscles. I had seen them through the glass but up close and personal they seem bigger.

His kisses are hot and probing. His tongue is almost down my throat. This is new for him, Kenny doesn't like to French kiss. His grip on my butt is hard and painful. He's squeezing me like he thinks I'm going to pull back. We are standing, and he has his fingers inside my panties. Alum tight or not, my juices are dripping. His fingers are slippery wet. He pulls them from my panties and smells them. That's new for him too, Kenny used to want no parts of the pussy near his mouth. He would never do that before.

He pushes me down on the bed, flips up my little miniskirt and grabs a hold of my panties. He pulls them off, but leaves my skirt, blouse, and shoes on. All he does is unzips his fly and flips it out. I don't even get to see it.

I have missed all of this man. I want to see feel and touch every part of him. But he's frantic, so I let him have me the way he wants. He tries to work it inside but I'm tight. Damn tight. He has to slow down. I hear him whisper that he forgot how tight my stuff was. He slows down.

He looks into my eyes like he's seeing me for the first time this afternoon. Now he kisses me like my Kenny with soft wet lips.

"Baby," I hear him say, "Baby I missed you so much."

He stands up and takes his clothes off. He is ripped up. Lumps of muscles are all over his lean body. He bends down to me and helps me out of my clothes and bra. We are laying in the bed, him on top of me and he is kissing my lips, then my neck, and now my nipples. This is how my Kenny does it. Now I feel him working on me down there. He is in my wetness and has got me opening to him. I feel him inside of me. As snug and as wet as I am, I am expecting him to climax soon as he gets it all in.

He doesn't.

He buries himself inside me and keeps it there. I feel his pulse inside

Emotional Drippings

me.

"My woman," he says, "this is my woman alone."

Then he starts to pump, and oh my God it feels like he is pulling me inside out. It's not painful, but I am so tight around him that it feels like he is taking my insides out with each thrust. I tell him to, "slow down daddy," and he does.

I feel his throbbing, his pushing and twisting, but no pulling out. It feels like he is part of me. I hear him say again, "my woman, my woman alone."

And the next thing I know, I am having multiple orgasms like crazy. I say like crazy because this usually doesn't happen with Kenny. I have never had multiples with him, but I'm having them now.

Like I said our thing isn't sex based, at least it wasn't. Every time he moves I have a climax. This is crazy. My mind tells me it's Kenny, but it's hard to believe because he is doing it better than my high school flame. After the multiples, I feel looser and a lot wetter. I tell Kenny to get back to pumping, and he does. And he pumps fast. Now when Kenny does it fast, it is usually over fast. I am expecting him to pop off any second.

I know this good fast pumping is not going to last. I usually have to slow him down to make it last, but he's working on me like it's going to last and damn if it ain't lasting.

He's not stopping, and he has me building up for a big one. If he keeps doing it fast like this, I'm going to . . . damn.

A big one, with Kenny?

What's really going on?

I wrap my thighs around his waist like I do my old high school flame and go buck wild because my man is giving it to me. I squeeze my thighs tight then I fling them open wide for him. If he's going to make love like this he can have it all.

I just had another blast of multiples and this ain't never happened with Kenny. I am cumming so much that I'm dizzy. I feel his sweat drops falling on me. I open my eyes because I have to look just to make sure it's Kenny and not my high school flame. He started a feeling building up in the nape of my neck that shoots down to my toes and causes them to ball up.

Damn, he made it happen twice. He's doing better than my high school flame. Oh, this is too strange. I feel him jerk a little inside me, but he pulls out me and says, "get on your knees."

Now I know it's about to end, he can't hang doggy style. He never has been able to. I get up on my knees, and he opens my thighs. He puts one foot up on the twin bed and keeps the other on the floor. He used to fumble around in the doggy position and not get it in right, but now he enters with no problem, and he starts off long stroking like he's not afraid of cumming.

Since he's going like this I push back when he pushes in, before he could never handle me meeting his thrust. We meet so many thrust that I am not trying to meet his thrust anymore because my man has beat the pussy up.

I collapse to the bed out of exhaustion. I am afraid to cum again. I'm laying flat on my stomach and he is still hard inside me, and he is moving. He is grinding into me hard and fast, and I feel him swell up and then I feel his whole body jerking on my back. I feel his hot warmth inside me, all through me. Natalie was wrong, very wrong about him popping off in only three pumps.

The door to the small room is suddenly pushed open, and a female

Emotional Drippings

guard is standing above us. She says, "Conjugal visits are over. Get dressed inmate."

Has it been an hour? I look the blue clock on the wall and see it has been an hour and fifteen minutes. Damn, my man threw down. When I roll over to kiss him, I notice his eyes don't leave the door. He says, "I love you." Then he is dressed and gone before I can put on my bra.

Now I know I'm dizzy and drained, but him leaving like that doesn't seem right. I get dressed, put my shoes on and walk out into the hall. Only Maxine and one of female guards are in the hall. I remember that Natalie has overnight conjugal visits, lucky her. We don't walk back through the shower room. It's a locker room that we are going through. The guard is looking hard at me and grinning. She draws her pistol and points over to the other side of the room.

I follow the pistol and see my man going into the room with the other female guard. One of her arms is out of her uniform shirt. The guard with my man is looking directly at me, and she mouths, "My man bitch," and signals for the other guard to take us out. I guess the other guard thought I was going to yell out because she puts the cold pistol to my head and tells me to keep quiet. Maxine saw what I saw, but she looks down and doesn't say a word either.

When I get on the bus, I'm not mad. At least my man ain't getting raped by another man. And whatever that guard is doing to him got him getting better at love making. Besides, in two years he'll be home with me anyway. So what if he's getting some pussy while he's locked up. She's a guard, so she'll probably keep him safe. This ain't a bad situation.

I'm not happy about the slut calling me a bitch, but she had watch to Kenny throw down with me an hour and fifteen minutes. That had to get to her. I can live with what's going on with them. He has to do what he has to do to survive.

Sitting on the bus, I can't help but wonder was it the alum or has he really gotten that good. Next month, I am going to have to go all natural and see what happens. Either way, it's going to be a visit to look forward to. Who knows, maybe the thing with my old flame won't last. When the bus pulls through the prison gates, I start to cry. I wish my man was free.

The End

Emotional Drippings

Bedroom Eyes

The first package he received was a single black rose. The note read, *it took me three weeks of tears but it's over now.* The relationship was over for Spanky three weeks before he moved out. He continued to live with Jasmine only because Rachel hadn't closed on her ninth floor luxury condominium. The day after she closed on the condo Spanky packed up his only suit case and one of Jasmine's and moved out of her suburban raised ranch home, which had been his residence for two and a half years. He left while Jasmine was at work.

While sitting at the bar at the Pizza Pub he told Oliver, his best friend, who was providing the ride from his old girlfriend to his new one that things had cooled off between him and Jasmine the day he met Rachel.

"It was love at first sight man. I ain't lying. I ain't never had a woman get all up inside my head like she is. It ain't never been this way for me. All I think about is her." He drained his shot in one toss. The drinks were on him since Oliver came all the way out to the south 'burbs to give him a lift downtown.

Oliver was pulling a Newport out of the box when he asked, "So was you still making love with Jasmine these last days?" He held the cigarette between thumb and index finger without lighting it.

"Yeah, as much as she would let me." Spanky grinned and beckoned to Rubin the blond Polish immigrant bartender who spoke ebonics.

Rubin catches the wave from the other end of the bar, "Yeah bro?"

"Hit us all around Rubin." Spanky emptied half of the frosted mug.

"Two more shots and brews?" Rubin asks walking to the tap and pulling two more mugs from over head.

"Yep," Spanky answers, "and frost 'em."

"So then she don't see it coming. I guess you kind of blindsiding her, leaving like you doing?" Oliver asks.

"Yeah, I guess so." He spins the mug on the bar top looking at it instead of Oliver.

"Damn dog . . . I thought she meant more to you than that. I mean shit man when she comes home she's going to be looking for you."

"I left her a note bro."

"Cuz . . . she provided you with a home for three years and all you left her was a note? In case you forgot . . . you was living in my basement until you met Jasmine. A person would think she would be worth a little more than a note."

The truth was he hadn't left a note; he only left her a voicemail after Oliver made his leaving sound so foul. He wanted to make clean break with no drama, no strings, and no clues as to where he was. That's why getting the cards and stuff tripped him out. Jasmine shouldn't have known where he was living.

When he got the first note, he was going out to walk Ming, Rachel's miniature white Poodle. The doorman gave him the note with the black rose. When he asked who left the note, the doorman described Jasmine to the t. - down to the dimple in her chin. He looked up and down the block and saw no signs of her. While he was walking Ming through the park, two birds shitted on him.

The first one got him on his bare shoulder, the other on the top of his head spoiling his fresh twist. All he had to wipe the bird mess was Ming's plastic poop bag, which had no absorbing qualities. The poop bag merely smeared the bird mess down his arm and onto his wife beater.

Ming squatted and took a dump right in front a beat cop, so he had

Emotional Drippings

to use the bird mess stained poop bag to scoop up Ming's crap. When he got back to Rachel's building, the doorman told him the water would be off for five hours. He washed his body and his hair with bottled water. He blamed Jasmine's black rose for the bird poop. She and her rose jinxed him.

Two days later, the second note arrived Fedex while he was lounging leisurely looking at television. The couch had arrived the day before and he positioned it across from the glass wall facing the fifty two inch LED flat screen which the television techs had just mounted. He was getting the hang of the remote when the Fedex driver tapped on the door.

He walked the package into the kitchen. The flat envelope contained the engagement ring he'd brought Jasmine. It was a quarter carat diamond ring he bought used from the pawn shop. The ring was taped to a note which read; *I believed you when you said you would love me forever because you were telling me the truth.* No sooner than he placed the envelope on the kitchen counter, his knee buckled and he dropped the remote and stepped on it; smashing it while trying to keep his balance.

"Damn!"

He swept the pieces of the remote up from the stone tile of the kitchen floor with the plastic bristled broom then limped back to the couch. At one time he did love Jasmine, but now . . . she was just a jinx. He went back to sit on the couch and rubbed his knee. When he gave her the ring, he thought for sure he would love her forever; but then he met Rachel, and things changed. It wasn't his fault. After his first kiss with Rachel, Spanky was hooked and hooked bad.

He limped back to the kitchen counter and retrieved the ring and the note. He'd gotten the ring by saving money from the loads of scrap metal he'd hustled up with Oliver. He bought the ring with his money, not hers, and he was proud of that fact. So much of what he owned came from her and other people. Not the ring, he bought that on his own.

He wasn't as fortunate as Oliver who went to work at the mill two days after high-school graduation. Spanky didn't have a daddy that worked at the mill. Through most of high-school he lived with his grandmother until she died and his mother moved in her house with her new boyfriend. After his grandmother's funeral he moved in with Oliver and his dad. It was Oliver's dad who showed them both how to scrap metal which allowed them pocket money.

Once Oliver got on at the mill, his daddy moved back down south and left him the house. Oliver gave Spanky the basement rent free. With his mill job, house, and metal scrapping money, Oliver became a sought after bachelor. With only metal scrapping money and no job prospects, Spanky became the broke buster that lived in his best friend's basement, until Jasmine.

He met her in a grocery store parking lot. She had a flat tire, and he changed it for her. Doing something for somebody, especially women in need, made Spanky feel good about himself. He asked the pretty damsel in distress to lunch, and she accepted.

He took her to an all you can buffet and went broke on taking her to the movies that same night. The next day was Sunday, she picked him up and took him to her church. She was twenty-four years old with a college degree and a job. He was nineteen and scrapping metal.

Jasmine was renting a house with an option to buy, but she didn't know how to start the lawnmower that came with it. Spanky kept Oliver's old truck running with duct tape and wire pliers and was happy

Emotional Drippings

to be living rent free in a basement.

After going out a couple months, he found himself doing things for her like fixing her washing machine, patching her garage roof, painting the kitchen, getting the squirrels out of her attic, and anything else that he could do to be helpful. And he did it all for no charge because he liked being there for her, and she did things for him too. She helped him study for his CVL, showed him how to register his metal scrapping as a business, and she changed his diet from carbs and fats to vegetables and proteins, Spanky told her, "We fill each other's holes." She urged him to want more, and he gave her common knowledge.

Knowing that she was a *real* church girl, he didn't pressure her for sex. He liked thinking of her as pure and better than the other girls he had been with. She was smarter, prettier, cleaner, and holier than any other woman that ever looked his way. So waiting for the sex was no problem, they were building something real.

He was going back and forth from her house to Oliver's basement for over three months before she let him spend the night, and all they did that first night was cuddle and kiss.

But, his first night with Rachel was a wet dream come to life: head, pussy, even anal. Rachel was a year younger than him but way more sexually aware. She called herself a sexual beast and Spanky found that to be true. At nineteen, he had only five women his whole life; Rachel had made and was still making porno movies. Spanky hadn't told Oliver that she made porno because he didn't know how to say it without making her sound like a . . . hoe.

He didn't know why her making porno wasn't a problem for him, but it wasn't. He was cool with the situation. He had even jacked off to a couple of her scenes while she watched. Her being a porn star was exciting to him. Matter of fact, everything about her excited him. Life around her was nonstop thrills.

Jasmine wouldn't even watch a porno, and she didn't want him watching them either. She said that they would distract him from a righteous life because they were evil. Rachel wasn't evil; worldly yes, evil no. She told him she earned fifteen hundred dollars a scene and more if she squirted. She always squirted when they had sex. She told him, "You MAKE me cum. That's why I took you from that woman." They did it twice a day every day.

He was lucky to do it twice a month with Jasmine, and afterwards she was always sad. "We sinning, and the Lord wants us to live right," which meant getting married, but she wouldn't marry him until he found a real job.

Rachel told him his job was making her smile and that the gods must be happy with them because what they did felt, "so damn good." Even her explanations excited him.

He'd met Rachel in the same grocery store parking lot where he'd met Jasmine. She was struggling with loading a bag of dog food in the trunk of her care. When he first went into the store, he helped an old lady load some dog food into her shopping cart too. To thank him, the old lady blessed him in a funny language and dusted him with some good luck powder. The powder made his eyes water, but he didn't complain to the old lady.

Spanky easily placed Rachel's bag of dog food into her car. When he looked up from the trunk, he noticed her breast had popped free of her halter top during her struggle with the bag of dog food. He couldn't help but stare, and she didn't immediately correct the exposure.

The small perky twins with pieced nipples seem to demand his full

Emotional Drippings

attention. Each nipple had a small gold hoop through it, and the hoops contrasted beautifully against her dark brown skin.

"Take a picture," she said.

"I wish I could."

"Why?"

"Cause I would look at it every five minutes for the rest of my life."

She laughed, covered herself, and invited him to lunch. She was living right around the corner from the store in a townhouse. She served him shrimps and cocktail sauce. Throughout her townhouse were portraits and pictures of snakes and snake figurines. The biggest snake picture was above the futon in her bedroom. She'd brought that picture to her new condo and again placed it above her futon.

Most mornings like this one, Spanky woke up looking at that picture. A gray and red snake stretched out the length of the black velvet picture. He knew it was the way the big picture was painted that caused the snake to stare at him no matter where he was in the room, but knowing that didn't lessen the eerie feeling of having a snake starring at him when he woke up.

This morning Rachel woke him up going out to walk Ming. He rolls over on the futon to wrap himself better in the sheet when he hears keys jingle. Neither his nor Rachel's keys jingled. There is one house key on a ring and they share it, and her car key is on the end of a pink rabbit's foot. It doesn't jingle either. He sits up on the futon and pats around. He finds his keys to Jasmine's house taped to a note which reads; *it's time to come home.*

He stands immediately up from the futon and looks around the bedroom. Then he goes into the walk-in closet and the bathroom. He searches the condo, but he is alone until Rachel walks through the front door with Ming.

He hasn't dressed and is standing in the middle of futon butt naked holding the keys and the note when she walks into the bedroom.

"Baby," he begins, "you ain't go believe this."

"Shhhh."

She drops to her knees in front of his thighs and takes him into her mouth.

Looking down at the tangle of jet black curls on the top of her head, he stops talking and inhales deeply through his nose and exhales heavily through his mouth. Morning sex is her thing, especially if she worked the night before.

After filming, she wants what he thinks of as bossy sex. The next morning, she gives orders and wants to be in total control, and it always starts with head that gets him harder than railroad iron.

This morning is no different. When he is stretched out too long for her **to** take down her throat, she orders him too, "lay on you back and don't move a fucking muscle, don't twitch, pump or pull, lay still. I'm doing all the moving this morning. Don't grab hold of me or nothing, and don't talk, don't call me baby or none of that shit. Just keep the dick hard, your mouth shut, and your hands to yourself. I will tell you when to open your mouth."

She mounts him without looking at him. Her head is back and her eyes are on the high ceiling which is stenciled with blue 3s, 6s, and 9s.

"Keep this fat dick hard nigga, you bet not nut."

He doesn't reach orgasm during bossy sex. This is for her not them. Rachel has orgasms during bossy sex, but he's noticed she doesn't squirt or get the rash on her chest like she does when they have sex for each other. This bossy sex is like her going to the bathroom, something

Emotional Drippings

she has to do to feel right.

At the start of the relationship, he found the bossy sex exciting until he started seeing her need and her tears. Despite the harsh talk, tears accompany her orgasms during bossy sex. And he's learned that they are not tears of pleasure. It's like she is trying work something free through fucking, and knowing that, he accepts her verbal abuse.

"Oh yeah that's it big daddy, mama got it coming now, oh yeah start pumping that log daddy, push up hard damnit, real fucking hard, make my teeth rattle nigga, fuck me like I feed you! Fuck me like you know I'm the bitch that put clothes on your back! Work this nut out of me, nigga, work it out!"

There is little pleasure in the act for him. She is going to and fro over his pelvic area like a child on a hobby horse until, "oh-h sh-h-hi-i-i-i-it," and she topples over onto the futon.

She lands on his arm that is holding the key and the note. He wants to touch her, hold her, but he is not sure what her response will be. They lay quite for minutes.

She rolls off his arm and asks, "Whose keys?"

He sits up. "Yeah I was going to tell you about those and this note." He hands both to her, "I rolled over this morning and found them in the sheets."

She reads the note.

"This is from that knock-kneed chick of yours and you found it in here?"

"On the futon."

"How? That means she was in here. Did you have that bitch up in here?"

"No. The note tripped me out as much as it's doing you. I searched the joint looking for her."

"How the hell did she get in here? Did she creep in on us while we were sleeping? Hell, I didn't get until three thirty this morning. This is some strange shit, Spanky. Damn, what we gonna do? We can't have that slut creeping up on us. We got to call the bitch."

"Huh?"

"Call the hoe, get this shit straight now. Ain't nan bitch gonna be up in my spot creepin'. Call her."

They walk into the kitchen for the house phone and as soon as he reaches for it, it rings.

"Hello, Mr. Spanky, your ride is down here waiting for you."

"My ride?"

"Yes sir, a Ms. Jasmine."

He turns to look at Rachel, "She's downstairs waiting for me."

"Huh?"

"She's downstairs."

"Well, let's go see the bitch."

Rachel slides into jeans, t. shirt, and leather slides. He jumps into a sweat suit and his flip flops. He opens the door and walks out first. Looking down he sees a line of red dust and rock salt sprinkled in the door way. Rachel sees the line, screams, and jumps back.

She snarls and hisses at the red dust.

"Who the fuck," she tries to jump over the line but is thrown back to the floor and lands on her back. She strips her clothes off and yells strange words at the dust. She tries again to cross the door jam and again she is forced to floor.

Spanky is tapped on his shoulder. He turns around to see Oliver and Jasmine.

Emotional Drippings

Jasmine blows a powder in his face that sets his eyes on fire. He falls to his knees in the hall. He blinks and wipes he eyes clear. Something is wrong with what he sees.

The hallway is tattered and old, holes are busted in the plaster, and the carpet is soiled and worn thread bare. When he looks into the condo, he sees a withered old lady with flat sagging breast and cruddy feet. He looks around for Rachel, but only the old lady and squirrel looking dog are in the room. He notices the gold hoop earrings in the nipples of the old lady's flat breast. The old lady is sitting in the middle of a bunch of mirrors and a big picture of a snake is hanging from the ceiling. She reaches for the door and slams it in his face.

Oliver bends down to him, "She hexed you bro. I thought something was twisted when I dropped you at this dump, but I wasn't sure until I saw her. When I came back a week later to tell you that my daddy died the desk clerk told me about her. She's a witch man, and she be getting young cats all the time. I couldn't get to you because I had to tend to my daddy's stuff, so I told Jasmine."

She bends down to him, "I didn't believe him baby. I am so sorry. I thought you both were trying to play me some kind of way. But then I saw you walking that little rat dog and looking like a pick-a-ninnie about the head, I talked to the desk clerk, and he told me the same thing he told Oliver. And then I saw her wretched behind, and I knew Oliver had spoken the truth.

"So I went to my pastor, and he sent me to his wife who gave me this stuff," she holds up a little bottle filled with red and white crystals and another bottle of brown powder, "and with the desk clerk's help we were able to reach you baby.

"I love you Spanky and Pastor's wife said it would only work if you loved me. You can see clear now and I can too. You are my man, and I am not going to let a dried up witch take you from me."

Oliver stands up, "We got to go, y'all, before she hexes us all." He helps Spanky to his feet.

Spanky looks at the tattered closed door; he wants to kick it open to get another look at Rachel, but when he looks down and his dirty pants and the run over house shoes on his own crusty feet he says, "Damn, get me out here!"

Spanky no longer sees the desk clerk as a suave doorman with dreadlocks. He is a hunched back wino who needs to comb his hair.

"No mo' bedroom eyes, young brother? So you seeing clear, huh? Remember, it ain't just here, da magic is everywhere. Now run boy!"

The End

Emotional Drippings

Real Life

My name is Charity Lewis, and I am about to be a forty-eight year old freshman at the community college. This is my second time attending the school. During my first admission, I became pregnant with my daughter, Neale. I withdrew, had her, and went about the life of raising a child.

School wasn't an important thought of mine at the time; education took a back seat to day-to-day living. I have always been a hardy reader. Whatever is close gets read, so my education hasn't stopped because I'm not in school. However, school education wasn't a "priority" like the young admission clerk said a few minutes ago. Feeding my daughter and keeping a roof over our heads and clothes on both our backs were the priorities.

On the few occasions when returning to school was a thought, I also thought about Neale's father, Hurston. We met here at this school. He was a nice looking young man, not real attractive but not ugly either. Hurston was ten years younger than me.

I was a twenty-eight-year-old freshman the first time I enrolled. Even though I had very good grades in high school, going to college right after graduation wasn't what was expected. I did what everyone else in my family had done and found a job. I ended up working for an industrial spool manufacturing company until my back was injured.

The county hospital doctors told me right away that I would never be able to lift anything over twenty pounds without straining my back. The doctors at the spool company didn't see it that way. My lawyers had to fight those people for eight years to get compensation, and the money they finally settled with wasn't enough to keep a kitten in catnip. But with that money, and my monthly disability check, and help from

Mr. Brown, Neale and I have made it through. Now my child is going to college, and she has me going back to school too.

The school tried to get me to register online because I am registering late, but this mature student couldn't really follow all the on-line prompts, so I came up here to get help. The young admissions lady has been really nice. She told me a lot of students my age have been returning to school and most of them prefer to register in person.

The problem wasn't my computer literacy; the problem was the confusing on-line directions. She smiled at me saying that and said she understood. She left with my registration card in hand, and that was twenty minutes ago.

She has a nice bright office to work in. It looks like she shares it with four other people. I see four desks with those little movable walls separating their workspace. I have never worked in an office. I imagine it would be nice work, clean and all. One young fellow has two people sitting at his desk, two young ladies, and one of them is popping gum. Lord, I wish she would stop; it sounds and looks so ignorant. A person would think that since she's trying to register for college she would put her best foot forward. Maybe she doesn't know any better. Who knows, but I sure wish she would stop popping that gum.

The truth be told, I wasn't on my best behavior my first time either. I got in school because I sent a picture to a contest the local paper was having. The contest was for a picture of a Chicago place or thing. I took a picture of a light-pole on a corner, and it got an honorable mention. A photography professor from school contacted me about a scholarship for photography students. I wasn't working, so this sister jumped at the chance to go to school for free. I came up here with the attitude that these people owed me something because they recruited

Emotional Drippings

me.

The only class I attended regularly was photography. I loved taking pictures back then almost as much as I love reading today. My father had given me a Polaroid camera when I was a kid, and I started taking pictures the minute he gave it to me. Neale draws pictures, and she is good, a natural artist people say. It's because of her drawing that we are both in school.

Neale won a scholarship to a fancy art school down town, but she refused to go unless I enrolled in a school as well. She got the bright idea after she came across the old photography portfolio the professor had me put together. She kept questioning me until I finally told her about the contest, the scholarship, and getting pregnant with her. Well, the child took my leaving school personal as if she had something to do with it. I told her she was the result of a decision that she was not part of. My saying that didn't faze her a bit.

The next thing I knew, the girl started messing around on our computer, and she found me money for school, a scholarship for returning students, and a government grant. I thanked her but said no; all that stuff was behind me. And I wouldn't have come back to school if she hadn't threatened me.

Before Neale found out she had the scholarship, she had plans to go to the army after she graduated. She hadn't enlisted, but the recruiter was hot on her trail. The man was calling our house daily. Neale understood perfectly well that I didn't want her in the army. My fear for her or any woman in the service has been a topic of conversation since she was a toddler. She threatened to go to the army and forgo her scholarship unless we were both going to college. Neale is hard-headed enough to have carried out the threat, of that I am certain. So the same reason I left school got me back in school, Neale.

"Here you are, Ms. Lewis." The young lady has come back to her workspace and handed me my schedule. I like how she has her hair; those natural braids look so healthy. There are extensions in my braids, but only until the perm grows out then, this sister is going to go all natural like my daughter and her friends.

I have registered for five classes, the same five as before: English Composition, Algebra, Physical Science, American History, and Photography. Looking at the schedule, I'm searching for the professor's name who got me here twenty years ago. I didn't think it would be there after all this time, but what catches my eye is the English teacher's name, Kaplan H.

Hurston's last name was Kaplan. Couldn't be, but to make sure I ask the young lady, "Do you know the English composition teacher's first name?"

Hurston and I meet in composition class. He was an English major hoping to get accepted into a university. He'd applied late but was still hopeful. The day I was going to tell him about being pregnant was the day he found out he was accepted in a school. He was so proud and so looking forward to going to the school. Not wanting to be his doom cloud, I said nothing about being pregnant.

I was twenty-eight and he was eighteen. If the pregnancy was anyone's fault, it was mine. He deserved a chance at life without a child slowing him down. I was attending college on a fluke. He was there following a plan. Who was I to mess that up? So, he never knew about Neale.

"Sure Ms. Lewis, no problem, his first name is Hurston. Dr. Hurston Kaplan. He teaches here and at a university. We're real lucky to have him here. You'll like him. All the students do."

"Oh, I'm sure I will."

I leave the bight office without saying another word.

*

Outside in my little white Corolla, I ask the air, "What are the chances of that?"

I don't even start the car. I can't.

"What are the chances? Oh my God, Hurston. Hurston is teaching at this school. Oh my God. This really shouldn't be happening; things have moved past this. My life and Neale's life is past this."

I never told her that her father was dead. I told he left and couldn't come back, and that was good enough when she was little. When she was around fourteen, I told her the truth that her father didn't know she was born, and I didn't know how to find him.

She accepted that answer with no more questions because a couple of her friends had gotten pregnant, and she began to see how real life happens. At about sixteen, she got it into her head that Mr. Brown was her daddy in spite of me telling her that he was just a friend of the family.

"Yeah ok, if that's what you two want me to think," was her reply to the truth. She had evidence, "Look Ma, you are short; me and Mr. Brown are tall. Ma you got honey brown skin; me and Mr. Brown have fudge brown skin. Ma you have thick lips and kind of big ears; me and Mr. Brown have small ears and thin lips. You can say what you want Ma, but I know who my daddy is."

The two of them do favor, and they favor enough to have some ignorant folks talking awhile back. And that little, nasty, envious, untrue, and long living rumor was confirmation for Neale. A couple of

30

years ago she started giving Mr. Brown Father's Day presents, and he added coal to the fire by happily taking them, "Oh that is just what I wanted Baby Girl." I settled with the fact that if she wanted to think he was her daddy, and he didn't mind so be it, but now her real father has surfaced.

"What am I going to do?"

I wonder could there be more the one Hurston Kaplan in this city. It could be more than one. Before making such an assumption, a sister should be sure. Reaching to the back seat, I grab the fall catalogue of classes. Flipping through the pages, I see that H. Kaplan is teaching an African American Literature class right now. I will just slide by the classroom and peep in. Recognizing him shouldn't be a problem.

*

This isn't a hot day, but suddenly I feel overheated. I don't mean to rush through the halls, but I can't help it. Rushing through the crowded halls is what I am doing. I have to see if it is him. Room 238 is the room: 210,212, 218, 224, 232, there it is 238. I take a deep breath and blow it out slow before I reach for the door, but before I can grab a hold of the knob the door is opened. Standing right in front of me is Hurston. I'll be a monkey's uncle. I lower my head immediately.

"Good afternoon, are you in this class?"

"No, I'm sorry. I have you tomorrow. I registered late."

"Oh, ok, we will see you tomorrow. I was opening the door hoping to create some type of circulation. It's a bit stuffy in here."

He is saying all that to my back because I am making a speedy get away. I feel his eyes on me. If I turn around, I think I would catch him staring at my butt just like he used to twenty years ago.

"Excuse me, Ms."

31

Emotional Drippings

I hear him calling, but I am moving. At the stairs, I take them down two at a time.

*

Back in my car, I start it and flee. What am I running from? I don't know, but running is exactly what I am doing. The question that slows me down, is whether I am running from something or to something - from the past or to the future? I don't know.

After I park in front of our building, I realize I am running to my daughter. I have a strong desire to see her, to be in her company, and to maybe tell her something. It's a childish feeling, like when a kid knows her teacher is going to call home. I have to tell Neale something before someone else does. But what and where do I start?

When I enter our apartment, she is typing on the computer. The computer is in the front room of our two bedroom apartment. We both use it, so putting in her room or mine didn't seem fair, so we put it in the front room, and that stops both of us from going overboard. Mostly, it stops Neale from overdoing it because there is nothing on the internet that will have me up at two in the morning like it does her. If I didn't stop the child, she would live on that thing.

"Hi, Ma."

She doesn't turn from the screen to greet me.

"Hey, baby."

"How did it go? Did you get registered?"

"Yep, without a problem."

"Get your books?"

I forgot the darn books.

"No, I forgot. Hey, I want you to go to classes with me tomorrow if you don't mind?"

Where that came from, I don't know, but it is a good idea. I do want her to go. I want them to see each other, and once they are together the three of us will work it out from there. This is too much for me to handle on my own; it's a three people situation. If all three of us get together, the situation will work itself out. Walking over to the computer, I bend down to kiss my baby on the check. She is my baby even if she is a foot taller than me.

She looks from the computer screen to me, "Are you ok, Ma?" My child has always been able to sense when things are not quite right with me.

I tell my baby, "Yeah, I was just thanking you for getting me to register for school. I think it's going to change our lives."

She shrugs her slender shoulders and goes back to typing. We both are wearing pink spaghetti strap tops. She has cut hers in half to show the whole city her flat belly. Mine is the full length it was designed to be. Not that I couldn't wear a belly shirt, my stomach is flat thanks to a hundred daily sit-ups. I do fifty in the morning and fifty at night. I chose not to show the whole city my stomach because I am the mother of a young adult daughter, so I dress like I have that responsibility. It looks like she is on the art school's website. She is setting up some king of student account. I kiss her again and ask, "So, do you think you can go to school with me tomorrow?"

"Sure, I would like that, being supportive of nervous freshman is a good thing." She says with a smile. She has no idea how nervous I am.

In my bedroom, I collapse across my sleigh bed with street shoes still on. Oh how I love this bed. It was purchased because the sales clerk acted like a sister couldn't afford it. And he was right, I couldn't. But damn if that was something he should have known. The man

Emotional Drippings

categorized me on the spot, and that irked me beyond my belief. The money that was in my bra that day was the down payment on a new used car, but it bought me the sleigh bed and respect, or so I thought.

When I came home and told Mr. Brown what happened, he laughed at me, and told me I fell for a salesman's trick. He said it's the salesman goal to sell product even if he has to anger me into buying it.

Mr. Brown said, "The end result was you brought a bed with money that was earmarked for a car. So who won, Lil Bit?"

After he laid the facts out for me, smoke was coming out of my ears. The salesman pegged me and played me. I went back up to that store and got my money back. Neale and I went and the found the Corolla that afternoon. However, when I got home, the sleigh bed was in my bedroom. Mr. Brown brought it for me at half the price, and he couldn't wait to tell me the story.

"After the salesman lost your business Lil Bit, I knew he was going to be frantic as a hound to make a sale. I went in the store and fumbled around. I didn't even look at the beds right off, and when I did look I checked out the real expensive ones. After awhile, I picked out a big one that cost a couple of grand. We were at the cash register when I pulled out my bankroll to pay for the big bed. Teasing him a little, I told him we'd better measure the headboard because it looked like it might be too wide for my bedroom.

"We measured about four other headboards until we got to the sleigh bed. Of course I told him it was the right size, but I acted like I had no interest. As I was walking out the door, I told him to save myself some time that I would buy the one that fit if he could work with the price. We haggled until he knocked off half the tag price. And that Lil Bit, is how you got a Christmas present in July."

34

He still had a Christmas present for me that year, like he has for the past twenty-one years that I have been living in this building. One would think the amount of time he and I have kept company that we would be a lot more serious about each other – at least living together. But that's not the case. He lives back there and I live up here. We would be a lot more serious if he wanted to be more serious.

It's funny because people think it's me stopping us from being a real couple, but he's the one that doesn't want to give up his freedom. He likes living back there with his cat and his whiskey. He's set in his ways just like his old mangy tomcat.

Him and that cat both come and go and live as they please; they are two old stubborn rascals. I tried to be friendly with the cat, but he hisses at me every time I try to pet him. When he gets locked out, I will open the door for him but he runs right by like he cannot stand to be near me. When Neale lets him in, he rubs all against her legs and meows for her to pick him up and pet. That evil old tomcat is friendly with who he wants to be friendly with. He hisses at me and meows for Neale. He does as he pleases and the same is true with Mr. Brown.

Mr. Brown doesn't wash his dishes until he feels like it. He doesn't get out of his bed until he's ready. He drinks as much whiskey as he wants when he wants. He dresses in them old timey clothes and thinks he's sharp. He gambles as much as he wants with nobody checking into his affairs, and he eats as much fried pork and sardines as his blood pressure will stand.

He knows if he had a full time woman, someone to look after him, all those freedoms would be gone. And when I do try to help him, say I remind him to take his medicine, he goes to fussing and carrying on like my concern is nagging. He hisses at me just like that old tomcat,

Emotional Drippings

and just like I do with the tomcat . . . I let him be.

With me, Mr. Brown knows all he has to do is offer a little help here and there, take me out to a play or a movie, buy me some books and magazines, and he will get some female company every now and then which is how he wants it, every now and then. It's been that way since the beginning, and I am not complaining at all.

We started being friends a year after Neale was born. She was sick one night, constipated something terrible, and he showed me how to use a piece of soap and my finger to get that hard booboo out of my baby.

I didn't think much about him because he was so much older. He was in his fifties then, but he kept coming around with what I needed: light bulbs, pearl earrings, milk, a winter coat, toilette paper, a tennis bracelet, diapers, a oak bookcase, fresh mustard and turnip greens, a computer, and he could fix anything that broke in the apartment or on my car. He was and is real handy to have around.

One day, I asked him what he wanted from me. He said whatever I wanted to give him. I told him he was too old to be my man. He said, "I ain't tryin' to be nobody's man. I will help you the best I can until you find somebody that will help you betta. You my young tenda lady friend."

To Mr. Brown, I am still a young tender, and I like that too. Over the years there have been a couple of "somebodies" in my life, and he has never interfered with my dating, but it didn't take me long to figure out that most of those men couldn't or wouldn't do half of what Mr. Brown was doing for me and Neale, especially Neale.

Anything that girl asks him to do he will do. He bought her first bike and taught her how to ride. He taught her how to drive and bought her that beater with a heater of a car. And when one of the local thugs was harassing her, it was him who whispered something in the boy's ear that got him out of her life. He is not her biological father, but Neale is right, Mr. Brown is her daddy. Last week he showed me his insurance papers and she is listed as a beneficiary along with his legal kids; me or his past wives were listed.

Not being listed didn't upset me. What ruffled my darn feathers was that two of them children on the list were younger than Neale. I was a little salty behind that. Those two younger kids got me to seeing red because that meant he got some woman pregnant after he and I became friends . . . with his old ass.

I kick my street shoes off and swing my feet up on the bed. My mind is filled and starting to spin a little, jumping from situation to situation and person to person . . . Mr. Brown's kids . . . school . . . Huston . . . and Neale. How did I forget to buy my books . . . running from Hurston that's how.

Hurston looked good. He's still slim with a full head of hair. He was wearing glasses, but they added "character" as Neale would say. That's what she said about my few gray hairs, "They add character, Ma. Don't color them."

Sitting up, I look into the bureau mirror. There are only a few gray hairs, and if they weren't all clumped together they would go unnoticed. I have no wrinkles or laugh lines to speak of and only a little pudgy under my chin. No bags under my eyes at least not today. Overall, I am still a good looking sister. With these extended cornrows, more than one young man has ran up on me from behind about to rap until they saw that I was a grown woman, a veteran, they called me. "Man she's a veteran, but she got a nice booty."

Emotional Drippings

My butt is still firm and standing. I can't say that about my breast. They went south years ago. But the booty is still holding its own. It held Hurston's eyes today.

Hurston.

Hurston and Neale.

I get out off the bed and walk over to the window and look out for Mr. Brown's black Cadillac. I see it parked behind me. I slide into my house shoes which used to be Mr. Brown's house shoes and walk up front to the door.

"Where you going, Ma?" comes from Neale who is now in the kitchen at the refrigerator. The girl is all legs, and those cut off blue jean shorts she is wearing are way too short for my comfort. I have told her twice already; tomorrow they will be lost at the Laundromat.

"Over to Mr. Brown's."

"Be sure to tell him about my car pulling to the left, and the Men's Day celebration at church. Remind him that he promised to attend because you know he's going to try and get out of it." She says grinning.

Neale joined church all on her own. I'm proud of her for that. Despite my CME attendance - Christmas, Mother's Day, and Easter - Neale has become a regular member. I just wish she dressed more like a church girl.

"Will do," I say going out of the door.

There are two apartments on the first floor of our building: mine and Mr. Brown's. My mother told me that these old brown stones were once small mansions, but during WWII people divided up the space for renters. Mr. Brown lives in a kitchenette. I should say lived in a kitchenette because the old man is seldom home these days. His absence really shouldn't matter because I have had very little to say to him since I saw those younger kids listed on the insurance papers.

But, I need to talk to him now to get his advice on the Hurston situation and hear what he thinks about me taking Neale up to the school tomorrow. His advice is always so sound so matter of fact.

I knock on his door and push it open all at the same time.

He is sitting in his rust colored leather reclining chair with that evil gray tomcat in his lap. He hears me enter and turns his head toward the door and smiles when he sees it's me. The tomcat hisses. It is an ugly old thing.

"Hey, college girl."

I close the door behind me. He thought Neale bullying me into going back to school was real funny. We laughed for a good while, but that was before I found out about them younger kids.

What Mr. Browns tries to do is talk about pleasant stuff and not his mess. He tries to get me laughing when I should be angry. Usually, I go along with him, but a sister needs to know about those darn kids. My intentions were not to come back here and bring those kids up; the needed conversation is about Hurston and Neale, but seeing him sitting there rubbing that – lives as he pleases tomcat - has made me mad. Along with the fact that he is wearing maroon and gray-checkered polyester pants with gray lace-up shoes, and a shinny maroon nylon shirt. He keeps on wearing those out-of-style clothes even after me and Neale bought him better clothes. His closet is filled with new jeans, dress pants, and shirts from past Christmases, birthdays, and Fathers' Days, but he won't wear them unless we insist.

He'd rather wear these played-out fashions. Large retail stores don't even sell those types of pants, shirts, or shoes. He has to drive all the

Emotional Drippings

way out to the suburbs to buy those old-timey clothes, and the man who owns the store is just as old and stubborn as Mr. Brown. It's crazy; an old-timey store filled with old men buying discontinued fashions like they are shopping at a high fashion boutique.

I am standing here, staring hard at Mr. Brown and that cat, searching my mind for the right words. I didn't come back to talk about those kids. I need his advice, and this is not the time to argue.

"Lil Bit, why is you standin' there like somebody snatched a hold of your bloomers? What ails you?"

"You ail me." The tone is nasty even to my ears.

"Huh?"

"You and those kids born after Neale ail me. Where did those kids come from, Mr. Brown?" It is a direct question, but I will bet a fifty dollar bill to a doughnut that I won't get a direct answer.

"A grown woman like you knows were babies come from, don't cha?"

He's grinning now, showing his top silver tooth and his bottom gold one. Only a truly ignorant person would have one gold tooth and one silver tooth displayed in their mouth for the whole world to see.

"Don't play with me, Mr. Brown."

"Lil Bit, I showed you them insurance papers to make you happy, not to get you all riled up."

"Well, I am riled up, and I want to know where those kids younger than Neale came from, and where you been sleeping because you ain't slept back here in a week."

This is not how me and Mr. Brown talk to each other. This tone is the one that comes out when I am angry with Neale. I hear my foot tapping on the linoleum floor, and my arms have crossed across my chest.

"Girl what got stuck in your craw and sent you back here madder than a wet hen?"

"I have told you what is bothering me, Mr. Brown . . . those kids and where you been sleeping."

The grin is still on his face, "Lil Bit, them is my grandkids."

"What?"

"My grandkids, Lil Bit . . . I have two grandbabies." He is still grinning and petting that hateful cat.

"But they have your last name?"

"My daughter ain't married. She's too evil a woman to keep a man." Now he is looking at me like he just said something clever, trying to call me evil on the sly.

"Well, where have you been sleeping?" the question sounds a little silly and real jealous, two things I am not, but I am still riled.

"Lil Bit, I wanted to tell you this in my time but looks like it's goin' to be your time." He reaches out and grabs a hold of my hand and pulls me close. "I got prostate cancer. I been stayin' over night at the VA hospital because of the chemo treatments. The only time they had available was the evenins', and since the treatment drains my strength they arranged for me to stay over."

He's looking at me hard . . . trying to read my thoughts which he thinks he can do. The big grin has left his face, but a slight smile is lingering, "When you get to acting jealous?"

I don't want to be acting jealous. I was simply curious about where my friend was. "Ain't nobody jealous of your old self." I drop his hand and go to the kitchen table and pull up his only kitchen chair and sit on the side of his recliner.

Emotional Drippings

Cancer, Mr. Brown has cancer.

"How is the treatment going?" I can think of nothing else to say. I have known no one who has gotten better from cancer. Sure I heard about people living with it, but I personally know no one who has survived the disease, no one, and now Mr. Brown says he has it.

"Aw, it ain't going that good anymore." He sighs and runs his fingers across his shaved head. He sighs again. "They told me today they think the cancer is spreadin', so they stopped the treatment."

He looks at me straight on. And I see the whites around his brown eyes are strained and red. He is tired. He looks down.

"Hey, you know I am glad you came back here. I want to give you somethin'." From the end table on the other side of the recliner he picks up a folder. "This is the deed to this buildin'. It has been willed to you."

He doesn't own this building.

"You don't own this building, Mr. Brown."

"Who owns it then?"

"The Brown Reality Group."

"I am The Brown Reality Group." He's grinning again.

"Mr. Brown, maybe you should pull out the bed and stretch out a bit. Want me to pull it out of the wall for you?"

The treatment must have affected mind.

"How long have you been taking the chemo treatments Mr. Brown?"

"Off and on? Oh, a number of years, yeah a good number. The cancer started in my spleen, and they thought they had got it all, but it is in my prostate now, and the test they had me take a while ago said maybe my kidneys too.

"I got to be honest with you, Lil Bit, all this testing and treatment got me kinda slow and real tired. I'm kinda glad they got me goin' into the hospital tonight that will give me a chance to rest up good and build up some strength. I don't like feelin' this weak. Open that folder like I asked you."

He doesn't look as sick as he says he is. Yes, I have noticed a little ash on his normally healthy dark skin, but I thought that was from him halfway taking care of himself. I didn't think he was sick.

Mr. Brown doesn't get sick, no more than his blood pressure. That is what he has talked to me about, his pressure. He has never mentioned cancer before. I reach over and grab his hand this time. The cat hisses and jumps out of Mr. Brown's lap to the linoleum then up to the kitchen counter and out the window.

I hold Mr. Brown's one hand with my two. His hand looks older than the man I know he is. This hand doesn't look like it can turn a wrench, drive a nail with a hammer, paint a bathroom, wash my car, tote my duffel bags to the laundry, or squeeze my butt just hard enough to make me want to do it. Mr. Brown's hand can do all that. This hand looks like an old man's hand, not my Mr. Brown's hand. What did they do to him in a week? My Mr. Brown doesn't get sick; he eats what he wants, and he drinks when he wants and doesn't get sick. But this hand . . . this hand looks like a sick man's hand.

"Don't cry, Lil Bit. Stop that, it's not as bad as all that."

I don't like crying. I don't like it when my body does something I didn't know it was going to do. Mr. Brown is wiping the tears from my cheeks.

"When you go to that hospital, you better do exactly what they tell you. Don't be having Neale bring sardines, pig feet, and all that kind of

Emotional Drippings

stuff up there. You got to get better. Neale needs you to fix that raggedy car you bought her, and she is expecting you to go the Men's Day program in a couple of weeks, so you can't be messing around at that hospital. Go in there and come right out."

I am crying too hard now. I have to leave. I stand and tell Mr. Brown, "I'll see you later. What hospital?"

"The VA, here take the folder with you."

He puts the folder in my hand as I turn to leave. I turn back around and kiss him. I kiss him hard and long. I want him to know I care about him.

"You get better, Mr. Brown. You get better quick." His hand is squeezing my butt again.

"Lil Bit, it's nothin' but tests and rest, don't worry yourself like this."

"Ok," I answer, but I know better.

Mr. Brown is sick. I pull his apartment door closed behind me. I should have known. He doesn't stay away like he was doing. I should have known.

Entering my apartment I hear the shower running. Neale is getting ready to go skating. I close my bedroom door and fall across my bed. The clock reads one thirty. It's been a hell of a morning. I should get up and put those chicken breast in the crock pot.

I don't.

What I really should do is drive Mr. Brown out to the VA Hospital. I stand up with that on my mind and go to the window to make sure his Cadillac is still outside. I see a Medi-car, and Mr. Brown is climbing into the side door. He has arranged his transportation. Mr. Brown takes care of his business, he always has.

The folder he gave me is on the bed. I pick it up and open it. It's a deed at least it looks like a deed to me. Behind the document is a letter written to me in Mr. Brown's horrible hand writing.

He says he wishes he could have left me more, but with three ex-wives, nine children, and grand children he had to spread the pie kind of thin. He is also leaving the care of the tomcat to me. He tells me he loves me and Neale.

Mr. Brown is not expecting to come home from the hospital. I cry myself to sleep.

*

I am having a crazy dream. It's not a dream but more like a memory. I am reliving every date I had with Hurston. The first one at pizza place, the second at the show, and then the various hotel rooms we rented. The crazy part is that on every date I am wearing red, and somehow Mr. Brown shows up right before me and Hurston kiss or get sexual. I didn't even know Mr. Brown back then. I didn't move into the building until Neale was a month old. And I didn't wear red until after meeting Mr. Brown. The color was too bold for me, but since he liked me in red, I wore red.

When I wake up, the clock reads six thirty, and the shower is still running. Neale must have left the water on. I burst into the bathroom to see Neale in the shower, and her morning toiletries on the sink. I leave the bathroom without disturbing her. The computer clock screen six thirty-five. Oh my God, I have slept a whole day away.

*

Once dressed, I get on my knees and say a needed prayer for guidance with the Hurston and Neale situation, and I pray for Mr. Brown's health. We load into Neale's roomier car for comfort. While watching Neale drive my mind drifts to Hurston.

45

Emotional Drippings

What will he think of me?

How will he react to Neale?

How will she react to him?

I still haven't told her about Mr. Brown.

I can't do this with Hurston . . . not today.

Today, I need to be with Mr. Brown. Mr. Brown needs me. He needs me and Neale. What am I thinking? I need to be at that hospital.

"Mama?" Neale's eyes are on me. "You're crying, what's wrong?"

There is no sense in not telling her.

"Baby, the man teaching my English class is your biological father. My plan was to have you two meet today. But something more important has happened. I found out yesterday that Mr. Brown is sick with cancer. And baby, I would rather see him today than go through the situation at the school. Don't get me wrong, it's important for you to meet your father, and believe me you are going to meet Mr. Hurston Kaplan just not today. I think we should spend this day with Mr. Brown if you don't mind."

Her face twists up as if she is in pain, "Mr. Brown is sick? I knew something was wrong. I felt it all inside of me. I knew something wasn't right. But Mama, Mr. Brown don't get sick, Mama, you must have it wrong. My daddy don't get sick. Where is he Mama?"

"At the VA Hospital, get on the expressway and I will direct you from there. Do you want me to drive?"

"No, my car is pulling a little bit to the left. My daddy has to fix it before I let anybody else drive it. He showed me how to accommodate for the pulling when it happened on the other side. It won't take him long to fix it. You know how fast he fixes stuff once he gets started."

*

Tony Lindsay

At the doorway of his hospital room, we two are standing waiting for a technician to pull some type of machine from Mr. Brown's room. When the tech and machine exit, we walk in. Mr. Brown's eyes are closed. He is sitting propped up by pillows.

"Hey, Mr. Brown," Neale says pushing past me to get to him. Mr. Brown opens his eyes and turns his head to face us.

"Hey, Neale girl. How you get way out here?" His voice is barely above a whisper, but his smile is big. For some reason, after all these years, I actually like how his top gold tooth looks with the bottom silver one. Neale bends down to kiss him on the cheek and forehead.

"Who is that behind you? You brought your mama out here." His eyes are smiling. "Lil bit, didn't you have school today?"

"I start next week. I only registered this week."

He looks at me with narrowing eyes. "Mmph, I thought you was registering late and classes started this week."

"Well, you just thought wrong," I say bending down kissing his other cheek, "you don't know everything." He's slipped his hand around to grab a hold of my butt, and he has a nice grip on it too.

"Lil Bit, gal, I loves you and Neale."

"We know Mr. Brown," Neale says, "We love you too."

"I'ma love y'all till the end. I had to take small steps with you, Lil Bit. It took me the better part of ten years to get next to you." The smile fades from his face as he nods asleep. His head raises and he says, "You know it must be some strong stuff in that shot they gave me cause I'm getting kind of tired.

"Lil Bit, these people out here crazy. They sent in a man nurse to wash me up this morning, and I was suppose to let him wash my privates. Shoot, I ain't that sick. Before you leave, Lil Bit, I want you to

47

Emotional Drippings

help me wash up some."

His head lowers again, but he wakes up before it goes all the way down.

"It's good to have folks around that care about me. Some people leave here with nobody they love close. That's not gonna happen to me now because y'all here. Will you look over yonder there. How did y'all get my old tomcat pass that mean ole nurse?"

We turn to look, but there is no cat.

"That mean ole nurse would not give me another Jell-O, and Neale you now snuck my cat by her. I'ma have to watch you girl, you getting slick. Come here boy, ain't he fine? This old gray cat been my friend for over twelve years. Hold on, boy. Don't leave, let me get you some sardines."

His grip release my butt, and he exhales such a long breath that I don't want to look down at him. Mr. Brown is gone and I know it.

The monitor beeps continuously, and the room is flooded with hospital staff. There is nothing they can do. Neale knows it too. We hold each other's hand.

In the car Neale says, "He was a real good man and a real good daddy. I will never have another daddy. I don't need one . . . you understand me?" She is looking at and through me.

I understand she's hurt that's what I understand. After awhile, she will want to meet Hurston Kaplan, so tomorrow in class I will reintroduce myself and tell him about his daughter. We will take small steps as Mr. Brown would say.

"Baby, that's fine. That's fine, baby."

The End

Melody's Night Out

The bar was packed. A small ten stool establishment with three tables, Terri's usually only housed the regulars on Thursday night. It was the place that the *twenty-somethings* of the neighborhood frequented. The shoulder to shoulder crowd was due to a regular, Mike, winning the Chicago State University spoken word contest. When he made his acceptance speech, he mentioned that the party would be at Terri's, and that filled the place with rappers, spoken word artists, and poets.

"Damn girl, this joint ain't seen this many people since dollar drafts and two dollar shots."

Melody was stepping out of the red lighted entrance way into the small bar. She and her best friend Drena remained steps away from the full body of the crowd.

Over the rumble of the bar she heard Drena saying, "Not even then. Terri's has never been this crowded. I think that's Mike and Curtis at the other end of the bar."

Melody felt Drena on her heel and towering over her from the rear. Which is how it has had been since the third grade. Drena has always been at least a foot taller than her. They stood steps away from the entrance door feeling the warmth from the summer night's air at their backs and the coolness of the air-conditioner before them.

"It always stinks in here."

"It's a bar Drena. It's supposed to smell like this."

"And when are they going to upgrade those ghetto speakers? All you can hear is the bass. Are we going over to the guys or what?"

"Yeah, I was just trying to see what was going on before we just popped up on them."

Emotional Drippings

Melody was looking at Mike's corn-rowed head and Curtis' shinny bald one. She and Drena had been hashing over a plan since last Thursday night. It started with Curtis' recent marriage announcement and Mike's admitted attraction to Drena.

Since ninth grade Mike and Drena had been, "looking at each other," but neither one of them said anything or did anything to move things past the "looking at" stage. Their inactivity was usually due to Drena having a boyfriend or Mike having a girlfriend. Last Thursday night though, Mike changed that.

He point blank told Drena that he thought she was fine and that they ought to quit playing with each other and get something started. Drena, who was out of school for the summer, not working, and no current boyfriend, told Melody that she was definitely flattered and interested.

Melody's situation with Curtis was different. He was about to be married, and she wanted her attraction toward him known before that happened. He had not expressed any interest in her whatsoever. She on the other hand thought Curtis was, "one of the most beautiful chocolate brothers with Asian slanted eyes that God created."

He first took her breath away when he was the new kid at their high school. He tried out for the basket ball team and got the starting forward position. She was already the lead pompom girl. They went to the same parties and hung with the same people, but their personalities never permitted them to be friends. He would either snap off on her or she would snap off on him.

They couldn't hold a conversation without arguing, and it had been that way since day one. Despite their personalities not jelling, she was still very physically attracted to him. And she wanted him to know that before he got married. So Melody and her best friend came up with a plan to get Mike and Curtis over to her place.

"Are you sure I look all right? Maybe I shouldn't have worn these white pants."

Melody still had her eyes on Curtis at the bar.

"You been knowing Mike since we were kids. Stop worrying about how you look. He seen you when you was butt ugly and running up and down the alley with snot hanging out your nose. So stop tripping. This is still your 'hood. People know you here. He knows you. Y'all only been out in the burbs what three or four years? Quit acting you brand-new to the 'hood and what's happening around you."

Melody didn't turn to face Drena while she spoke because the bartender had gotten her attention. Carlene, the gapped tooth bartender, with thirty-eight double D's, was leaning toward Curtis while serving him his drink. Through her leaning, she had put her bustier under his nose. The ivory camisole she wore exposed her cleavage to those who looked, and Curtis looked. Melody wanted his slanted brown eyes on her, not Carlene.

"Seven, it's been seven years since I lived around here. We were sophomores when I moved Melody. And I ain't acting like I am brand-new to the 'hood. I am just a little nervous about the situation. Mike and I might be moving from friends to something a little deeper."

Melody shifted her round brown eyes from the bartender to Drena's narrow dark brown face. She grinned up at her showing her freshly whitened teeth.

"Yeah right deeper. You may want to feel something deep, but we both know all you trying to do is move from friends to temporary fuck buddies. When school starts back, Mike and y'all's little fling will be

Emotional Drippings

history."

No sooner as the words left her mouth Melody regretted them. She watched Drena's cheerful expression turn serious while she considered her comment. Her best friend had always been sensitive, but as of late, with no man in her life, she was extra sensitive about relationship comments.

Melody saw the dismissive flick of Drena's wrist, along with the return of a small smile, and she knew that she wasn't insulted. Drena smoothed down nonexistent wrinkles from the front of her white linen dashiki and said, "Hopefully we will start a little more than that girl, so you're not at all nervous about having Curtis over your place?"

No, she wasn't nervous about getting him over her place. The plan would work just fine, but what she was worried about was saying the wrong thing and getting him mad, or him saying the wrong thing and pissing her off.

"No I am not nervous, but come on let's get over there before Carlene smoothers him in her titties."

She stepped into the crowd and Drena followed. Elbows were shoved, shoulders were bumped, booties were touched, drinks were spilled, conversations were over heard, cologne was smelled, and perspiration offended; as Melody led them through the crowd.

"Girl, if another one of these artistic types steps on my toe, it ain't go be no crowd in here, I'ma scatter all these smart Negros."

Melody closed her arm down firmer on the purse under her arm. It wasn't the bruised toes, as much as it was the closeness of the crowd that truly frustrated her. Being a woman of small stature she was often pushed aside in crowds. And that along with all the persistent bumping, and uninvited touching of her thighs and butt was pissing her off. She wore the short yellow and black jersey skirt to attract Curtis's eye, but her exposed skin left her vulnerable in the breath sharing crowd.

"If you wouldn't have played in your head for an hour, we could have got here on time."

She heard Drena's complaint, but she had to spend time getting her hair right. Just because she wasn't nervous about the proposed rendezvous didn't mean she wasn't going to look her best. She had a perm which meant her hair had to be rolled nightly and styled daily. Drena's short Afro-centric twists were wash and go as far she could tell.

Melody paused, allowing Drena to her side.

"Ain't no *on time* at a bar, this is not a show lounge."

"Oh there is an *on time*. We getting our toes stepped on because we're late. The *on time* folks are sitting at the tables and the bar with un-assaulted feet."

After the tousled navigating, Melody did want a seat. Mike's was surrounded by congratulating peers who were dressed in baggy jeans, gym shoes, and white over-sized t-shirts. They opened their group when the ladies approached.

Mike and Curtis exchanged dap, and brief hugs with the guys in the group and bade them farewell. Melody wondered why Black men just didn't say goodbye instead of all the ceremony. The group's leaving left space for them to step closer to Mike and Curtis.

Mike turned sideways on his barstool.

"What's up ladies!"

He greeted them loudly over the music and chatter of the crowd. Curtis simply nodded his head to their arrival.

Melody answered their greetings with a request.

"Ain't you nice gentlemen going to offer two ladies your seats?"

Emotional Drippings

She saw the drink in Curtis's hand and watched him down the shot. He then turned his bald head to the left, then to the right and asked, "What gentlemen and what ladies? Ain't nothing but thugs and chicken-heads up in this piece," he stated with his eyes roaming down her deeply v'd yellow chiffon blouse. "And some nicely dressed chicken-heads at that."

Melody's felt her forehead squishing into lines, and her nostrils flaring. She knew arguing upon greeting each other was what she and Curtis always did. She wanted this night to be different. But she heard the words coming out of her mouth despite her thoughts.

"Chicken-head! Nigga, is you drunk already. And get your motherfuckin' eyes off of my titties. Damn!"

When he looked up from her blouse, she saw his eyes widen and his face squinted into a querulous expression.

"Huh? What titties? You mean your nipples. Cause that's all you got is nipples." He rocked his head toward Carlene, the bartender. "Now those is titties."

Melody crossed her arms across her chest and hacked out, "Fuck you, awight?"

She turns her back to Curtis, exhales, and gives Mike a completely different expression. She smiled warmly and asked, "What about you slim, are you as ignorant as your buddy, or are you going to lead by example and offer a lady your seat?"

Melody wondered how many shots they'd had while Mike drained his shot glass. He growls from the burn of the liquor. She was thinking that maybe Drena was right, and that they were too late. Curtis and Mike could have gotten too drunk to play. She watched Mike's rapidly blinking his eyes and wiping moisture from his forehead. He looked up from the shot glass to her.

"You see baby it's like this . . . by you asking for my seat that negates my offering. If I give you this seat now all I would be doing is succumbing to another overly aggressive Black woman. And I ain't about that right now, maybe later after this . . . what is this we drinking, Curtis?"

"Granddaddy."

"Right, Granddaddy. Now after this Granddaddy kicks in, I might give you my seat."

Melody straightened her posture and stepped back a bit from Mike with her arms still crossed over her chest.

"Overly aggressive Black woman? Is that how you see me Mike?"

He nodded his head yes. "Melody you bossy as hell, and you spoiled. Ain't none of that a secret." He put his fist up to his mouth and covered his belch. "Sorry."

"Bossy and spoiled, oh I see now, both of y'all must be drunk."

"Yo ass is bossy, and you mean. A skinny *eeeviiil* ass woman."

The way Curtis sang the word evil, almost made her laugh. She turned to him as he continued with "You scare little kids with your wickedness."

She waves her hand in front of her face as if wiping them both from existence.

"Yeah y'all drunk, but you know what?" She pointed to Mike and said, "Ya mama!" Then she pointed to Curtis and said, " And yo mama too! Keep the fuckin' seats. You broke ass niggas is trifling fo' real. I don't even know why we stopped over here."

Curtis attempted to imitate her dismissive wave and almost toppled off of the bar stool. Melody bit her lip to stop the laugh.

Emotional Drippings

Regaining his balance on the stool, he managed to say, "Keep it moving mommy. Those two white boys at the end might give y'all they seats."

He leaned his head toward the end of the bar, and Melody noticed the only two white people in the tavern.

"Oh no!" Drena interrupted, and raised her hand in protest. "I know good-and-well you ain't sending us to the white man? I know you two strong Nubian brothers are not going to leave chivalry to the hands of the oppressors. You're not really sending us down there are you? Mike really?"

Both of Mike's hands went up in an act of surrender.

"OK! Hold it! Shit that's enough. A brother is just trying to get his drink on. Here just take the damn seats, come on Curtis. Let's go out to the truck and blaze up. I got with the cush man right after I cashed the prize check."

He winked and grinned towards his buddy. Melody sees the brightness of his teeth reflected in the mirror behind the bar.

"Cool, I got Swishers in my pocket."

Curtis rose from the stool, and Melody saw the sly smirk on his face. "Here you go chicken-hea. . . I mean ladies."

Mike and Curtis changed places with the two friends, allowing them to sit on the stools.

"Y'all dressed nice. What's up? You two usually be bummed out like everybody else in this place on Thursday night. Where the jeans at? What's popping with the fly dashiki, slacks, the miniskirt, and heels?"

Melody heard Mike's question, and was happy he noticed that they had dressed up a bit. But she decided to leave answering it up to Drena. Maybe she wouldn't sound as angry, and bring about a better mood between them.

She saw Drena looking critically at Mike's and Curtis's jeans, gym shoes, and over sized Red Fox and Tupoc t-shirts. And remembered that Drena thought sagging jeans and oversized t-shirts were a "degrading statement of the prison indoctrinated system that we live."

Melody decided that the four needed a break from each other.

"Wasn't you going out to kill some brain cells or something? Why are you still here?"

"Damn, take a brother's seat and dismiss him, ugh?"

"What, you want a thank-you for doing what's right?"

"Nope, not from you, Melody. Let's move out, Curtis, befo' she blows my little drunk."

She hoped the angry mood would change if they were apart. She said nothing as the buddies turned to leave.

Mike turned back around and said, "We'll be back, and I got something for you Drena."

He winked, laughed and stumbled half a step or so backwards.

Melody more out of reflex than intent put up her hand with all five fingers spread apart and said, "She don't need your Link card, she got groceries."

Mike steadied himself with Curtis's assistance.

"I know she got groceries, Drena got the *thi-i–i-ckness*." He smacked a kiss in her direction. To Melody he said, "You the one looking all malnourished and crackheadish."

She sat erect in the chair, and heard herself thinking 'don't say a word', but heard out her mouth, "Crackheadish. . . ump . . . ain't your daddy on the pipe?"

"What!" Mike attempted to step to her.

Emotional Drippings

Curtis grabbed his arm and redirected him.

"Come on man, we ain't got time. This is your night bro, don't let the wicked wretched one spoil it for you."

Melody nodded her head in the affirmative.

"Listen to your boy because you really don't want to go there."

She unzipped the purse in her lap.

Curtis pulled Mike from Melody and through the crowd.

Melody heard Drena exhale deeply and saw her run her fingers back and forth across the top of her twist.

"Why would you say that about his father?"

"Upmh, because his daddy is a damn crackhead, he knows it, and everybody in the 'hood knows it. His daddy comes up to our cleaners looking tore up from the floor up. Almost every day, he be asking my daddy to let him sweep up in front of the store."

"Knowing a thing doesn't mean you speak on it."

"He started it. I just finished it." She said zipping up her purse. "Besides the only reason you saying something is because he said he's got something for you."

"No, I'm saying something because you were rude."

"Damn . . . you know him winning that contest kind of throws a wrench in our plans. All these people ain't supposed to be here. They kind of change the whole mood of the place."

Melody looked around at the crowd shaking her head.

"You don't think calling his daddy a crackhead and calling them both broke ass niggas might have affected the mood?"

Melody spins Curtis' empty glass on the bar.

"No, they use to me talking to them like that."

Turning completely around on the stool facing the mirror Drena asked, "So are we still going with the plan?"

"Hell yes! We getting you laid by that spoken word nigga tonight."

"Oh so it's all about me, you ain't trying to get with Curtis?"

"Girl since high-school, you know that. I just can't believe he's marrying that gang banging Kania. That bitch is dangerous fo' real. Didn't Mike do her gorilla looking ass high-school?"

"How would I know that?"

"Who knows? Who cares? I just need the chance to tell Curtis how I feel. We're working the plan. That is if his flip ass mouth doesn't change my mind, and stop me from giving him something that will stay on his mind for a life time."

"A life time? What you got the Sunshine coochie?"

"Hell yes. Didn't you know that?"

Carlene approaches and clears away Mike and Curtis's glasses and places two napkins in front of them.

"You ladies drinking or talking all night?"

Melody ordered, "Two Cosmopolitans and two shots of Gray Goose with cranberry juice chasers."

"You know Mike and Curtis are probably not coming back over here once they come back in."

"I know, that's why we gonna go to them. We're going out to the truck when we finish these drinks."

"They're smoking weed in the truck. Suppose the police come?"

"Then you won't get laid."

*

Alcohol bold, Melody walked up to the passenger window of Mike's fifteen year old Chevy Blazer and tapped on the window. He didn't roll it down or cut off the noisy engine and rattling air-conditioner.

Emotional Drippings

Through the cloud of smoke he exhaled, Melody saw his lip mouth, "What?"

"We need a lift to my place."

"We who?" he mouthed.

"Me and Drena."

Melody watched the driver's window roll down. She had to step back and fan the smoke from her face. Mike looked past her to Drena who waved from under the parking lot's spot light.

"Yeah, y'all come on. Get in the back Curtis."

"What about the party dude?"

"Later for that party cuz, open your eyes to what's real."

"Huh?"

"Nothing, just get in the back before Drena gets over here, and call Melody to the back with you."

Melody smiled at Mike's almost frantic sounding directions to Curtis.

"Come on, Drena, we got a ride," she called across the parking lot. She didn't wait to be called to the backseat. She opened the other door and hoped right in. She sat on a gym shoe which she tossed to the floor of the truck.

From the backseat Melody watched as Mike got out the truck and went around to the passenger side and opened the door for Drena. She liked that.

"So how did y'all get up here?" Curtis asked her.

"Cab," she told him. She gave him her best tip of her freshly whitened teeth smile, and established eye to eye contact. If Curtis was at all slow on what was happening around him, she wanted to set him straight as soon as possible.

With Mike opening doors and ordering his boy to the back seat, it was clear he was on the right page. But maybe the liquor and weed had clouded Curtis' mind. So she decided to be more obvious about the situation.

"Do you still hoop Curtis? I mean you look like you still do." She runs her hand down his arm, "All muscular and stuff." She scooted closer to him on the bench seat.

"Yeah I still play a little tournament ball. Nothing like our glory days though. When you was out there cheerleading, that was the shit. You know what I mean?"

"I was a pompom girl, not a weak ass cheerleader. Get it right boo."

"I didn't mean no disrespect. I loved you being at the games. You use to kill 'em that lil ole dress, just like you doing in that one."

His eyes had returned to roaming down her blouse.

"What are you looking at?"

If he said nipples, or made any reference to her small breast the plan would be aborted.

"Whatever you want me to be looking at?"

She liked that answer.

"Curtis, all we need is a ride. You might as well get that mackdaddy tone outta your voice. Ain't none of that happening tonight. What, did that weed go to your big head and little head?"

She leaned into him with her eyes still in his.

"My little head is a big head too. So what head is you really asking about."

He had caught on, and she was pleased.

The first car she saw that drove up on the Blazer had its bright lights on. The second car pulled up to the driver's door with lights out. The third car parked parallel to the Blazer. The third car was a box Chevy.

Emotional Drippings

Curtis sat erect and pulled away from her.

"Damn that's Kania's car!"

Curtis' fiancé quickly emerged from the Chevy followed by five other girls.

She ran up to the Blazer's back window and yelled, "I knew this Thursday night clubbin' was some bullshit. Ain't nan nigga got to go out every Thursday night unless he fuckin' somebody at the place. And I thought yo' ass was different. Look at you in the back seat wid a hoochie! Pull all of them outta that damn truck!"

Melody saw the spit spewing against the rear window from Kania's mouth.

"You better go out there and calm that Pit Bull of yours down because me and my girl ain't taking no ass whipping. Not this night."

She unzipped her purse and pulled the .380 from it as she watched the gang of girls getting out of all three cars.

"Damn Curtis, me and you got to get out there and talk to your wife-to-be before this turns ugly."

Things had already gotten ugly as far as Melody was concerned. Most of the girls had baseball bats, chains, or golf clubs in their hands. When Mike opened the door he was snatched from the Blazer by a group of girls.

Drena attempted to lock her door, but the power locks didn't work and before she could reach the manual tab her door was yanked open, and she was pulled to the pavement of the parking lot.

Melody opened her own door and got out firing her pistol toward the girls that yanked Drena from the Blazer. All the girls ducked and scattered. Mike made it to Drena, and threw her back onto the passenger seat. He ran back around and got behind the wheel. Melody slammed the back door shut and mashed her tab lock down.

Mike hit the gas and swerved around the Oldsmobile that had pulled in front of him. Melody rolled down the back window and shot at the scattering girls and their cars. Mike didn't slow down when the Blazer spun onto the Cottage Grove Avenue. He kept the pedal to floor for three blocks until they got to Ninety-fifth Street where he made a hard left.

When they passed the interstate 94 East sign Curtis yelled, "Take the expressway ramp. She's scared to drive on the highway!"

Mike sped down Ninety-fifth Street to Stony Island Avenue. He hit the strip pavement that led onto interstate 94 eastbound.

They had driven for ten miles on the interstate with all heads constantly checking out the rearview window without saying a word, until Melody said, "I truly hope you don't marry *that* crazy bitch."

Nervous laughter came from all.

Mike said, "I agree with her man, because all you was doing was sitting in the back seat of a truck with a chick. And she went ballistic fo' real."

Melody watched Curtis fumbling with his hands in his lap. He looked out the window then back to Mike then out the window again. He started to speak but closed his mouth. He opened it again to speak but said nothing. He lowered his head and sighed. He looked at her and said, "It was so many of them . . . you think she really would have . . . the rings are on layaway so . . . she's just . . . man I don't know. . . It's like she think everywhere I go I am fucking somebody. . . every Thursday night we have a fight about me going up to Terri's Place. She was always threatening to creep up on me. . . but I thought she was just talking."

Emotional Drippings

Melody shook her head no, "She's way pass talking Curtis. That woman is looking for a reason to hurt you. Her and her crew was sitting in the lot waiting for you to do something. She been stalking your ass. Either she's crazy, or somebody been in her ear strong against you. And that's real talk. She ain't the one to make wifey, unless you want non-stop drama in your life."

Melody dropped the .380 back in her purse and zipped it closed. She saw Drena's cheeks twitching. It looked like she was trying not to cry and losing the battle. Her sobs filled the truck, and the tears leaked down her face.

"Oh hell Drena, I didn't think to ask. Are you ok? Did they hurt you?"

Mike flips on his signal and attempted to pull to the shoulder of the expressway.

"No don't stop! Take me home please. I am at the next exit. Please just take me home."

"Did they hurt you Drena?" Melody asked from behind her.

"No. I'm fine except for the fact that those girls just tried to kill us. They would have beat us with their bats and chains if you would not have had that gun. Other Black woman would have stomped us to the ground. And for what, because we setting in a truck with her man? They would have killed us for that? Lord Jesus take me home."

"I'm sorry," Curtis mumbled.

"It's not your fault Curtis." Drena said looking out the window.

When they were almost to the Indiana state line she said, "This is my exit here Mike."

Melody watched her as she continued to wipe tears from her face.

"You like living out here?" Mike asked her.

Tony Lindsay

"Please Mike I don't want to talk, just take me home."

The truck remained silent except for brief driving directions from Drena until they pulled into the half circle driveway that put them in front of the columns of her parents' home.

"Looks like your pops is still doing alright with his law practice. I remember his little office on Ninety-third in Cottage Grove, and y'all living above the store front. That was a minute ago huh?"

Melody watched Drena open the door of the Blazer and not slow down for the conversation Mike attempted.

She climbed out of the truck. "Thanks for the ride Mike. Melody call me when you get home." She closed the truck door and said nothing to Curtis. She went up the three steps and through the large columns and tall door without one look back.

Mike drove out of the circular driveway onto the street that led them out of the gated community.

Melody and Curtis remained in the backseat as Mike headed the truck back toward the city.

While they were on the expressway Curtis asked, "You mind dropping me at my mama's? I don't think me going back to Kiana's place is a good idea."

"You think?" Mike chuckled. "What about you Melody, where can I drop you?"

She saw him looking at her through the rearview mirror and his eyes; his eyes made her feel safe, as if he was looking out for her, protecting her through his glance and that made her smile.

"Six blocks down from the bar, I rent the first floor from my folks."

"Yeah, I forgot that your people brought the Jamison's two flat after they moved down south. So you got you own spot now, all grown up,

Emotional Drippings

huh?"

"I been grown for minute sir." Was that flirting she asked herself, no, just stating a fact.

"Yeah, we all gettin' older." Mike answered with his eyes on the highway not in the mirror.

"Yep, that's right," Melody agreed. "No time for the type of foolishness that happened tonight." She looked at Curtis who stared out the window silent.

When they got back to the Southside Mike asked her, "You don't mind if I drop Curtis first do you, his mama is right around the corner?"

Melody started to tell him that was because he drove past the exit that would have allowed him to drop her first but she didn't. She said, "Nope, that's fine."

When they pulled in front Curtis mama's house she thought about warning him again and said, "Remember what I said, she ain't the one Curtis."

And she realized that she wasn't either. Watching Curtis reduced to fumbling in the backseat of the truck changed him in her eyes. Good looking man he still was, but she had seen him weak and that lowered her attraction to him.

"I hear you," he answered avoiding her eyes, "see y'all later" he attempted to close the truck door but Mike stopped him.

"Hold up Curtis, Melody get up front with me, you ain't getting chauffeured through the 'hood. What do you think this is?"

With Melody in the front seat they both watched Curtis climb the stairs into his parents' frame house. After he got in Mike didn't drive right off.

"Hey, you know you saved our lives tonight." He said looking up at the row of amber street lights.

"You drove us outta there, so I didn't do it by myself." She adjusted herself in the seat.

He cut the engine off, "Drena was pretty shook up."

Looking out the passenger window Melody noticed a full moon over Curtis' house.

"Yeah, she takes things to heart. She don't understand the hardness between people, especially Black people, she thinks we should all just get along."

He looked from the lights of the dark block to her, "You don't think that?"

"I know better. Shit happens everyday."

"You know I want to tell you something, something I ain't bothered to tell nobody else because it ain't they business, people just ignorant."

She saw his jaws tighten all the way up to his temple.

"You see . . . my daddy ain't a crackhead . . . people think he is because of how he looks but he ain't. He suffers from depression. I just wanted you to know that. He's a good man even with the sickness. And I appreciate your pops letting him do errands around the cleaners. That gives him a reason to get up and out the house. I just wanted you do know that."

Damn, she thought, not a crackhead. She was one of the ignorant people because she truly thought he was.

"I'm sorry, Mike. I wouldn't have said that tonight had I known."

"I know that girl. You was just bein' you, trying to come off hard, I see through you. You got a nice heart."

She saw him lean toward her, she didn't move as he kissed her on

Emotional Drippings

the check. "That's for saving my life," he whispered.

Face to face, with eyes in his, she decided to kiss him. When the kiss ended she said, "That's a 'thanks for saving my life kiss.' I don't know what that little peck you gave me was."

He leaned toward her again, she felt his hand on the back of her head and his lips pressed firmly against hers. His tongue opened her jaws and found her tongue and started a dance. He leaned over to her seat and hugged her tight during the kiss. She relaxed during the embrace and found herself hugging him too.

The kiss ended, much too soon in her opinion.

Face to face, again she saw strength in his eyes that was unnoticed before, the hardness, the manliness. How had she missed it all these years? He moved in for another kiss, and she allowed it. His lips moved from her lips to her neck. She exhaled and pushed him back.

She looked him in the face again and said, "I thought you said you had something for Drena?"

He exhaled and didn't utter a word. He returned to his seat and started the Blazer. They drove block after block in silence. When they got her house his silence remained.

She turned to him and said, "If you want to come over tomorrow, in the daylight, after we both had some time to think about what almost happened, you can. That way we will both know if it was more than the moon light and the shootout that got our engines running."

She saw the drab look leave his face and a smile appeared.

"Are you sayin' that I got your engine running?"

She felt her own smile raise in her cheeks.

"Yeah that's what I am sayin,' but I don't know if what we was feeling can last past a night. I mean between tonight's action, the drinks, your weed, we had all kind of things working on us.

"My friendship with Drena means more to me than one hot night with you. If there is something real between us it will be there tomorrow."

He faced her with the smile still on his face and even his teeth looked strong to her.

"You felt something right?"

"Yes I felt something."

"Then why can't that be enough for tonight? I mean something is moving between us now. You right. It might not be there tomorrow, and that means we would have missed the experience. You know like me, tomorrow ain't promised. We got something hot going on right now.

"We wasn't thinking about a picket fence with each other, at least not to my knowledge, but we did spark something. And I say we should move on that spark and see how long we can keep it hot."

He ran his finger down her shoulder to her wrist and the stroke caused her shimmer.

"Come her girl."

She lets him pull her into another embrace and kiss.

"See," he breathed out, "this feeling right here needs to be maintained. We need to keep this going."

He guided her hand to his lap where she felt him straining against his jeans.

"The experience is now, not in the morning."

She lets her hand linger in his lap, "try to keep hot?" she asked.

"That's what real."

She felt his fingers with hers in his lap. She heard his zipper and she

Emotional Drippings

let him guide her hand into his jeans.

"But Drena is my friend."

"And she will still be your friend tomorrow. This is between me and you tonight. We ain't doing nothing to her. We doing something for us."

It was so damn hot and throbbing to her touch, she tried to pull her hand out but he held her wrist in place.

She didn't even see him approaching with the kiss. He was just on her, all over her. She felt his hands on her thigh, her belly, her chest, under her skirt, at the nape of her neck, and lastly her nakedness. She hadn't worn any panties. To his find, she heard and felt his warm heavy sigh upon her neck.

"The time is now baby." He moaned,

"Are we going to work at keeping it hot?"

"Yes."

"You promise?"

"Yes Melody, I promise."

"Come on then."

She climbed out of the truck and waited for him to get his keys out the ignition and manually lock the doors.

She grabbed him by the hand and led him up her stairs.

Midway up steps she stopped and said, "You know I got a pistol nigga. You ain't seen crazy, Kania ain't got shit on me, play me if you want to."

She was very satisfied with the huge grin that came across his face as he swooped her off her feet into his arms.

"We gonna keep this hot baby, bet that!"

The End

Our Dance

It was Wednesday; hump night in my study routine. I was carrying six classes that semester and three of them quizzed on Fridays. I was as tired as a three legged dog and not in the mood for the nightly bull sessions that the fraternity house offered. I was heading straight up the stairs to my room when Scott beckoned me with a wave into the living room.

At the time, I considered Scott a friend, and it was because of his urging and my own desire to make connections for the future that I pledged the cliquish fraternity. As a student from a working class back ground, I knew my grades had to be in the top ten percent if I expected to earn an internship at a major corporation. My daddy sat on no corporate boards although the church board he did sit on was instrumental in keeping me in school, but the work of staying in school was up to me. And, it was my responsibility to make the right connections that would lead to a good future; thus, my pledging the cliquish fraternity.

That evening I joined the five other fraternity brothers that were lounging in the living room with Scott. The topic of conversation was dates for Friday night's dance. Timothy, a fraternity brother who was scheduled to graduate last spring, had finally earned enough hours to graduate. He, along with ten other delayed graduates, had rented the faculty banquet hall for a dance. I thought it all absurd; why celebrate failing to finish on time. None the less, I joined Scott on the sofa.

Timothy was a chronic slacker who spent his study time guzzling beer and watching internet porn. His grades were far below average, and he seemed totally unconcerned about his academic ranking. His cavalier attitude concerning his studies along with his perverted use of

Emotional Drippings

the internet made him one of my least favorite fraternity brothers. His date for that Friday night was to be a paid escort. That didn't surprise me; I doubted his ability to interact with an educated woman he did not pay.

He sat passing the escort's photograph around, and she was voluptuous to say the least. If breast size had anything to do with providing maternal nutrients, this woman could have easily fed every hungry child in Poland and Ethiopia. Her rates were printed on the back of the photograph. What she charged for one night was half of what my family's church sent me for a full semester's allowance. I simply smiled. I was past being shocked over the dollars my fraternity brothers spent on frivolous whims.

I sat there listening to their list of possible dates for Friday night, and I was becoming quite bored until Scott mentioned a different name. One never spoken of in the context they were speaking. Certainly they spoke of her when they conversed about academic achievers, and when they required tutorial help, but they never spoke of her in carnal tones. Scott sat back on the couch rubbing his crotch, and he spoke as if his conquest was certain. He cut his eyes over to me trying to gauge my reaction to his statement. My thoughts were masked behind my smile; this was why he delayed me. I sat a few moments before leaving, not wanting to reveal my true emotion. I left for my room avoiding more eye contact with Scott.

My plan materialized in thought before I hit the top step. Once in my room, I sat on the corner of my bed and smiled. I was certain the plan would end my friendship Scott, but intervention was a must. Brenda could not go on that dance with Scott. Perhaps, if he would have spoken of her with some remnants of respect, I would have felt differently, but his tone was guttural. I had to ask her to that dance before him.

I lay in my bed thinking of how to do it. I had two classes with her, but in neither class did we talk. In three years, I had said less than five words to her, but things were different, I would not have her reputation or person polluted by the words or actions of Scott. But even though I appreciated her poise, I had never approached her. And not for lack of desire, the culprit was lack of confidence.

Restful sleep was not to be had; doubt and insecurity tossed me all night. The smile that graced my face with the conception of the plan was replaced the next morning with a grimace of dismissal. Across the room was a red head freshman entangled in Scott's arms and sheets. She was sound asleep and snoring slightly. Scott winked one of his pale gray eyes at me and put his index finger to his thin lips and nodded towards our bedroom door.

The standard operating procedure when Scott had a girl sleeping over was for me to creep out of the room without waking the girl. How he convinced them to engage in sexual intercourse with me sleeping across the room was beyond my understanding. With my clothes in tow, I left Scott with his most recent conquest.

Waking to see the red head in Scott's arms reminded me of his sexual prowess. He had slept with a different woman almost every week of the semester. I had slept with none. Obviously, he knew what to say and when to say it. In the shower I wondered would a pretty, respectable, intelligent, girl submit to the same words? Would his Don Juan verbiage corral Brenda into his bed? None of the girls who I considered smart and respectable had slept over with him so far, at least not to my knowledge. I woke mostly to underclassmen and girls not

Emotional Drippings

from the University. My hope was that maybe girls of Brenda's caliber saw through his trite approaches, and that his bravado was ineffective against their intellect.

When I entered my second class of the day, statistics, I saw Scott positioning himself behind Brenda in a lecture hall seat. I wished for a lesser adversary: one not six feet two inches, one who didn't drive a sports car, and one who stuttered over his words in the presence of girls as I did. I was ready to surrender until Scott slung the gauntlet to the floor. Sitting behind Brenda he mimicked fellatio and pointed to her. Our fates were sealed; we were engaged in battle.

Willing my legs forward, I walked down the steps of the lecture hall to the row Brenda was sitting. I breathed in deeply and made my way to the seat next to her. While sitting beside her, I was mentally producing a list of our commonalities: we shared an African American heritage, we were both computer science majors, we both were in our third year, both of us were in the top ten percent of our class although she was probably in the top five percent, and we both used yellow highlighters.

The lecture was over before I could edit my mental list or garner any confidence from it. Brenda was packing up her book-bag, and Scott was kicking the back of my chair, and I was praying for a steady tongue. Ignoring Scott's kicks, I stood picking up her book-bag from the floor and hoisting it on my shoulder, and asked if I could walk her to lab. Her positive response and warm smile almost made me lose my footing. When I looked back for Scott, he was gone.

I often enjoyed lab, but never with the intensity of that day. Brenda appeared determined in my knowing that she was quite capable in lab. Having observed her from afar for three years, I knew she was capable.

We worked well together because we both listened to the instructor and each other, and since we were talking science, I didn't stutter once.

After ninety minutes of stammer free conversation, my confidence rose a bit; I asked her to lunch. She told me no. She was meeting a friend for lunch, one of my fraternity brothers. Scott. She was tutoring him in calculus. She zipped up her book-bag and told me goodbye and left me standing at the lab workstation. Divulging Scott's motive at that point would have been foolish, I would have appeared jealous and insecure. I had to gain favor in her eyes if I wanted her to go the dance with me and not Scott. I grabbed my book-bag and ran from the lab to the cafeteria.

Upon entering the cafeteria, I walked directly to Brenda and explained that since our next class was together it was only logical that I join her and one of my best friends for lunch. Her face was puzzled but she smiled and agreed. When Scott entered the cafeteria and saw us eating together, he smiled half heartedly at me and offered Brenda an excuse for not staying and left. I was overjoyed. I was winning. After lunch I immediately hoisted her book-bag up on my shoulder. She smiled and we walked to class together.

Again class ended before I could put together the words to ask her to the dance. I was perspiring, and my tongue was no longer steady with the confidence from lab and lunch. Brenda heard my increased breaths and asked if I was ok. I nodded my head to affirm my physical health, but mentally, I was wrecked. She traced her finger across her forehead indicating that I was sweating. I wanted to stand and leave because the words just weren't coming. I only wanted to protect her. No, that wasn't true; I knew my feelings went beyond protecting her. I had been watching the girl for three years afraid to have a conversation. But to get the words out of my mouth, I told myself that I was protecting her, and it was only for one night . . . not a life time.

She stood to leave and I reached out for her hand and asked her to give me a minute. It was only eight words: would you like to go to the dance. I breathed them out in one breath. Her smile was full and her eyes sparkled when she told me yes. If there was a bigger man on campus that afternoon, he was unknown to me. I was without a doubt the Big Man on Campus.

That night in my room, I prepared for the argument Scott and I would have. I would tell him that I had serious feeling for Brenda, and found his statements about her disturbing. I would also warn him never to speak of her that way again. I was looking forward to setting him straight; however, Scott slept elsewhere that night.

My mind was purely evil. The entire night I envisioned Scott in Brenda's room. When I could no longer stand the jealous, obsessed, and insecure thought, I got up and to Brenda's sorority house looking for Scott's car. It wasn't there. His car was parked two doors down at another sorority house. I cursed myself for the insecurity and doubt and went home.

Doubt didn't enter my mind as I buffed my only pair of dress shoes, nor did it enter my mind when I brushed down my brown suit. It didn't show its ugly head as Brenda and I danced the night away. It appeared after the dance when I witnessed Scott walk Brenda outside. Doubt fused my feet to the floor and told me of course she preferred him, I was nothing compared to him.

It was Timothy's big busted escort who freed my feet. She asked me where was my pretty girlfriend, and she said it had been years since she saw two young people so in love. My feet moved by themselves.

Outside, I heard Scott telling Brenda that she was right about me. I did require a challenge to get into action. He hoped he would find a woman that could read him as well as she had read me and one that cared about him as much as she cared about me. He told her he still didn't see what she saw in me, but if I was the man she wanted he was happy for her. He asked if he should tell me that they were friends from high school. Brenda answered no, saying that I might feel manipulated. Scott told her she had manipulated me by asking him to act as if he was interested in her. Brenda said no, she merely gave me the chance to be the man of her dreams.

I never told Brenda I heard her and Scott talking that night. However, remembering the event has given an idea for the inscription in her anniversary gift, out thirteenth, 'From the man of your dreams, Love Thaddeus.'

The End

Emotional Drippings

Payment Due

I wasn't expecting much from her, just what she owed me for washing her car and mopping her floors. My hustle was doing odd jobs for people in the neighborhood, and I would wait for payment. Waiting for payment was my biggest advantage over the competition. A lot cats was doing odd jobs in the neighborhood, but most of them wanted to get paid on the spot. I extended folks credit, and that kept me a long list of regular customers.

I would cut people's grass four times in a month and wait until the first or whenever they got paid to collect. Lena got paid every other Friday, and she usually had my money on the Saturday mornings following her pay day. I went over her house to take out her trash and mop her kitchen floor every Saturday, but every other Saturday was when she paid me.

It was a Saturday morning after her payday, and I was at her front door ringing her bell. Her door bell chime sounded just like the one I had my house. It was one of those with the three tone chime, ding-dong-ding.

When I told her that her bell sounded like the one I had at my old house, she looked surprised. She looked like a guy like me wasn't supposed to have had a house with a doorbell. A lot people think that a dude getting his hustle on in the 'hood is broke and has always been broke, so I didn't get angry about her doubting look. I was a little disappointed about getting the look from her, but I didn't get angry. I understood that folks look down on a fifty four year old man living with his mama and doing odd jobs for neighbors. Hell, I looked down on cats like that too, until I became a cat like that.

The truth was I had more in money in the bank then than I had when I was working. My mortgage was gone, my wife was gone, my kids was grown, my car and car note was gone, and I was living with my mama paying pennies for rent. I had been crack and alcohol free for two years, and most of my money went straight to the bank. I only spent money on things I absolutely needed. I wasn't broke but I wasn't right either.

That Saturday morning, it was misty and wet outside from the rain the night before. I turned the collar on my khaki work shirt up because the wind had a chill in it, and I pushed her doorbell again. From behind the front door I heard Lena yell, "Come on in Princeton, the door is open."

I pushed her heavy oak door open and walked in her Georgian styled home. I had hung the oak door for her a month before. The people at the home improvement store wanted to charge her two hundred dollars to install it. I charged her thirty bucks and a pizza.

When Lena's house was Mr. Porter and his first wife's house, I helped Mr. Porter add an additional bathroom to the first level. I was maybe fifteen years old at the time. Mr. Porter was a carpenter and contractor, and he spent a lot of time passing his knowledge of woodworking on to me, and to any other kid that would listen and hang around. Thinking back on it, I guess he got unskilled labor dirt cheap by teaching us kids parts of a craft.

Lena had changed all the furniture inside of the house. The way she had her crib decked out always put a pause in my step. Like a lot of Black folks she has a picture of President Obama hanging on her foyer wall, it greets you when walk in, but that picture is the only thing that's everyday in her place. When a person steps from the wood floor of her foyer to the plush 'sink in an inch' fuchsia carpet, right away you can

Emotional Drippings

tell the Lena has style.

There are no plastic covers covering her pink chairs, couch or love seat. Her white marble coffee table and all the other furniture have dark cherry legs and trim. On her cherry mantle, above her smoke mirrored fireplace, she has a white and gray egg on a gold stand. Within the mirrored fire place, she has two ivory vases filled with pink and gray silk roses. I liked her living room, regardless of my mama saying, 'Lena's furniture is make-believe highfaluting.'

My mama and the other older women on the block talked about Lena because she married Mr. Porter when he was seventy-nine and she was twenty-six. I wasn't living on the block when they got married, but I was back with my mama last year when Mr. Porter died. People were doing a lot of guessing and talking about him leaving Lena well off. I didn't know about all that. I knew she went to work at the hospital every day, so he must not have left her that well off.

Some of the older ladies on the block are widows, and for three years after Mr. Porter's first wife died, I think they were hoping that he would have looked their way. But he didn't. He went with the younger Lena. And that put a bee in their bonnets, and my mama's too.

My mama used to take Mr. Porter dinner on Tuesday nights and watch Wheel of Fortune with him. I don't think she has said his name in five years, but her and the rest of the widows all went to his funeral, and cried, and spoke of him as if he were a pillar of the community. But Lena, they didn't speak of her well, they called her a tart or a cheap floozy.

When I walked into Lena's kitchen I didn't see the mop, the bucket, or the hospital smelling soap she usually left out for me to mop with.

"I'll be down in a second Princeton. I need you to help me wash these blinds in the tub," I heard her shout down from upstairs.

I walked over to the bathroom, and looked in the tub and saw blinds soaking in sudsy water. I figured she must have started with the upstairs blinds first because none were missing from the downstairs windows. I was expecting to spend time mopping her kitchen floor, so doing the blinds wouldn't have interfered with my next job. That is if we had gotten to the blinds that morning.

I had knelt down to the tub and was rolling up my sleeves when I heard Lena scream out. The next thing I heard was the loud thumps from her tumbling down the stairs. I ran to the stairs and found her at the foot. She was entangled in sets of white and gray blinds.

She was attempting to free herself from the blinds.

"That man is trying to kill me!"

I looked to the top of the stairs but didn't see anyone. What man? I was about to ask, but I noticed that from tumbling down the stairs her house coat had unsnapped and her breasts were showing. Lena was usually dressed in a navy blue scrub shirt and scrub pants. I thought of the outfit as her Saturday uniform since that's what she wore every Saturday that I came over.

I didn't mean to stare at her breasts, but I hadn't seen a prettier pair in quite awhile. Matter of fact, I hadn't seen any breasts in the flesh in quite awhile. Whether they are on a twenty-four-, thirty-four-, or fifty-four-year-old, a pretty pair of breasts causes a man to stare.

"Stop looking at my titties and help me out of this mess," she was on the floor still tangled in the strings of the blinds.

I was a little embarrassed that she caught me in my school boy staring. I reached down and began pulling the vinyl blinds from her.

Freeing herself, she stood and didn't immediately snap her

Emotional Drippings

housecoat closed. Instead she pointed to the top of the stairs and said, "I felt like somebody pushed me down the steps. I brought down more blinds than this earlier and didn't have a problem. But if I didn't know that no one was upstairs, I would have sworn that somebody pushed me at the small of my back. That's why I screamed before I fell. I screamed from being touched. The touch startled me."

I was trying my best not to look at her nakedness. When she stood up, the snaps at the bottom of her house coat came undone and that gave me a full frontal view of her body. Lena was in good shape. Her stomach was flat and her breast was as full as birthday balloons.

"Maybe you had a muscle spasm from carrying the blinds while taking a step. You know muscles are tricky like that."

I stopped staring at her body and looked to the top of the stairs when she turned her head to me.

"No, I don't think so. You see others things have been happening in this house every since I made my mind up about something."

She smelled like the blooming lilacs in the neighborhood. She began to snap close her house coat.

"Pick up the blinds for me Princeton. I won't bother you with the foolishness that has been on my mind. I know Saturdays are a busy day for you."

"I'm never too busy to listen to a friend."

I bent down and started picking up the blinds and saw the smoothness of her shaved legs. Usually when I came over, Lena's whole body was covered in her navy blue scrub uniform. I had never seen that much of her skin before.

"You consider me a friend Princeton?"

"Yeah."

I wanted to say 'hell yeah' but I didn't.

I didn't because when I thought about Lena like a man thinks about a woman, I also thought about the doubting look she had on **her** face when I told that I once owned a home. She summed me up in that look, and I didn't think she was happy with the total.

Lena was a good customer who happened to be a good looking woman, a good looking woman who I checked out from a distance, and I was cool with admiring her from afar until I saw her naked.

I think her nakedness outweighed the summing-me-up look that was in my mind. It must of, because I heard myself telling her, "I hope you think of me as friend, because I been thinking of you as a friend for a long time now."

She smiled up at me. Lena is at least a foot shorter than me.

"I hope you not saying that because you just saw my titties."

She was still smiling at me when she said that, so I knew she wasn't serious.

"Lena, I'm fifty-four years old. I think I can judge friendships on more than body-parts by now."

I gave her a wink and a smile and watched her snap close the last clasp at the top of her striped housecoat.

"Good, then put those blinds in the tub and come join me in the kitchen for a cup of tea. I have something I want to run past you."

The adult Lena doesn't look much different than the fast mouth teenaged Lena, or the bubble gum chewing and big bubble blowing child Lena that I knew. She has the same dark freckles across her high check bones, the same tiny chiseled pointy nose, the same big brown lemon shaped eyes, the same thick pouty lips, the same black curly hair,

Emotional Drippings

and the same brown skin that is only shades lighter than her freckles.

I watched her turn and walk away, and my eyes glued themselves to her wide but firm caboose. Her hips caused the stripes in her housecoat to bow out and the stripes bowed back in once past her hips. With the blinds in my arms I realized my mood had changed. My mind wasn't on getting to my next appointment, or even on making sure Lena knew exactly how much she owed me for mopping her floors and washing her car. My mind was on Lena as a woman.

I imagined me and Lena climbing the steps to her bedroom and me unsnapping her housecoat and lifting her to the high-post bed I assembled for her last spring. I put the blinds in the tub with the others and swished them around in the warm sudsy water. I delayed leaving the side of the tub. I was trying to put my mind back on business.

I couldn't afford to lose Lena as a customer because of a foolish thought brought on by seeing her naked. If I made a pass at her, after she rejected me, she would tell others. And most of my customers are single women. If a woman doesn't feel safe, she will warn others. And Lena's warning could have been the end of my neighborhood hustle.

I had lost one life from not thinking. I couldn't afford to lose the half of one I had managed to put back together. I decided to keep my thoughts of Lena and my mood to myself. I would drink a cup of tea, get my payment, and leave.

When I made it to the kitchen, Lena had a ham hock and onions boiling down on the stove, and a bowl of red beans soaking on the counter. I sat at the kitchen table in the chair by the door. She brought over the silver whistling kettle and filled the two white and gold trimmed china cups on the table. She walked the kettle back to the stove, and again my eyes went to her wide hips. She returned and sat at the table with me.

"Do you believe in ghosts, Princeton?"

Now, that was a off the wall question. I did and didn't believe in ghosts. I didn't believe because I had never seen one. I did believe because of what happened with my father. Since we were sitting at her table having tea, and since I was trying to get my mind off of Lena as a woman, and she was thinking of me as a friend, I decided to share the story about my father with her.

"Well I don't know, but I will tell you this. After my father died, the door to his workroom would slam itself shut if I forgot and left it open. And house lights that were left on would cut themselves off. And my mama swears that the oven cut itself off too. She says she has not burned a pan of corn bread since my father died. Now, I never saw my father as a ghost while I was awake. But sometimes I used to dream about him, especially if I was running late for school. He woke me up from a sound sleep more than once."

It was all true, for a minute right after my father died things were real spooky around our house. And since I was only a senior in high school it tripped me out even more. For kids dead is dead. They don't know anything about ghosts and the afterlife, at least I didn't.

"Has your father ever touched you or your mother as a ghost?"

My mind went to her telling me she felt hands on the small of her back before she fell down the stairs, and I thought that maybe it would be best to talk against ghosts being real.

"Well, my daddy has been gone for some years now, and I not saying he was really there, or that I believed he was a ghost. I'm just telling you that some weird things happened in our house right after he died."

Emotional Drippings

She sipped her tea, and placed her china cup on table. I smelled the ham-hocks and onions and heard my stomach growl.

"Mr. Porter actually touches me."

She put those lemon shaped eyes on me and waited for my response.

"Touches you how?"

She offered me the sugar bowl.

"At first it would only happen while I was sleep or half sleep. I would dream about him caressing me, and the dreams would feel very real. But here lately, it's been happening while I am awake, and the touches are not as nice as in the dreams. I can be watching television, and feel him pinch my cheek or poke me in my side. Initially, like you, I thought the touches were muscle spasms. But I noticed the pricks and pains only came with a certain thought."

I scooped two teaspoons of sugar from the bowl and stirred and blew into my cup. I avoided her lemon shaped eyes but enjoyed the lemon scent coming from the tea. I did believe my father slammed his workroom door shut because that was what he did when he was alive. If I forgot and left it open, he would slam it shut to let me know it had been left open. But I didn't think she needed to hear that because she was thinking a ghost pushed her down the stairs. And I doubted that.

"Why do you think his touches hurt you?"

"It's because of what I'm thinking. You know he's been dead for over a year now, and I am still a young woman. I refuse to feel bad about thinking about a man. My husband is dead. And when he was alive I was good wife, but he's gone now or supposed to be gone."

She said thinking about a man. I heard her loud and clear.

"So because you thinking about a man, you think Mr. Porter is hurting you?"

If I was Mr. Porter, I would have tried to stay around her fine self too. But dead is supposed to be gone. She was right about that. I was thinking I would fight a ghost for chance to be with Lena; if I had a chance at kissing her pretty pair, a ghost wouldn't have stood a chance.

"I know that's what it is. When he was alive he was crazy jealous. The three years we were married was a challenge at times. If I looked in a man's direction he would pinch me or poke me. He'd say 'I'll be gone soon and you can do whoever you want'. He knew I loved him, but he was insecure because of his age."

I watched her push her long curly black strands of hair from her eyes. And thought about my mama's and the other widow's words. They said she married him for his money. Well, what else did he have to offer at seventy-nine to a twenty-six year old? I wanted to ask her had she been thinking about a specific man, but I have learned patience. She was talking, so I was listening.

"I married him for love and security. And he gave me both, people don't believe that we were in love, but we were. He died in my arms. Did you know that Princeton?"

She looked from her tea cup to me and didn't wait for me to answer.

"We were in the front room hugged up on that old couch, and he breathed his last breath after he kissed me."

If a man shared his last breath with a woman, he might just hang around. I was thinking that maybe she was right and Mr. Porter was still with her.

"That's why I had you haul all that old furniture out of here; it all reminded me of him and that kept me sad. I knew the neighbors were

Emotional Drippings

talking when they saw all the delivery trucks pulling up with new furniture, but I didn't care."

I watched her sipping her tea through her pouty lips.

"I wanted a fresh start. Out with the old and in with the new. Redoing the house gave me a new attitude. It gave me confidence, enough to go back to school and get my Associates in Business Management. After I started the classes was when the nice dreams with Mr. Porter started.

"It was like he was consoling me, helping me stay focused on school, and helping me with my loneliness. I did miss him real bad, and the dreams were so real. I felt his touch, his kisses, and his caresses."

She put the china cup on the table, and looked at me square on. But my mind was on how damn lucky Mr. Porter was. He was dead, and still able to come back and enjoy Lena's company.

"I needed those touches and caresses, better in a dream than not at all. Understand?"

"Yeah," I nodded my head, and I hoped she was saying what I understood. What I heard was that she hadn't had a living man touch her in a minute, and it was that time. Again I thought about fighting a ghost.

"But after I graduated, the dreams lessened. I figured that was Mr. Porter's way of telling me to move on with my life. I started working on a business plan, and without intending it to the plan revolved around both Mr. Porter and you."

"Me?"

I sat a little straighter in my chair, and listened a little harder.

"Yes you. You see, Mr. Porter's contracting company was left to me, but with him being the sole employee there is little for me to manage.

Then I thought about what you do. The service you provide to the community, and the more I thought about it the more I realized that you are a contractor. True you are not licensed and bonded, but you provide a billable service."

She reached into the kitchen chair next to her, and pulled up a folder. Across the top of the manila folder was the name, 'Small Jobs Professionally Done, Inc.'

She put the folder in front of me.

"Open it up."

I was about to pick the folder up and open it, but when I reached for it I felt a poke in my neck. A damn hard poke, the poke was so hard that I took a gasping breath for air. I coughed, and cleared my throat, but made no comment on the painful poke. I looked around the kitchen. There was only me and Lena. I started tripping a bit, but I calmed down by telling myself that talking about ghosts had me imagining stuff.

When I glanced at Lena, she seemed not to notice anything, so I grabbed the folder and opened it. I noticed the ham-hocks didn't smell that good anymore. A stale order was floating through the kitchen.

"As you can see, very little financial investment is required from you."

Lena picked up her tea cup, got up from her chair and moved to the one right next to me. After she made some adjustments for her hips in the chair, she pointed to the details of the plan.

"Your business isn't much different than his was. What you provide is less skilled, but you are being contracted. And since your clients are, well depending on what you decide, will be 'Small Jobs Professionally Done, Inc' first customers; I propose to make you a full partner. What

Emotional Drippings

do you think?"

If she had stayed across the table, and not gotten so close to me, I would have said no right then. I wasn't in any position to start a business. But with her being so close, and with her breast pushing so hard against the thin material of her housecoat, and with the strands of her curly hair hanging so pretty in front of her eyes, my thinking was weak. So what I saw in the papers kind of made sense to me.

She was offering Mr. Porters truck, tools, and garage space. I was to hire a crew, and Lena and I would expand the business together. In six months time she had us buying a new truck, and renting formal office and work space.

"Think about this, Princeton. Other people are coming into our community making a living off of cutting grass, shoveling snow, and doing odd jobs. Why shouldn't we capitalize on our own market? What you are doing as a hustle should be ran as a business, and expanded to include more than this neighborhood."

When I looked up from the folder, the expression on her face confused me. I saw hope in her eyes. No one had looked to me with hopes of anything for quite awhile. She was hoping I could help her with her plan.

My life didn't consist of plans. I got up every morning and found work. I hustled. She was asking me to do more, to be part of more.

"I can do this, Princeton. We can do this."

I looked at her very thin finger with its bright white fingernail tip as it pointed to a total in a column under my name.

"Your initial investment is nine hundred and fifty dollars. That will assist in licensing, insurance, and marketing materials. Will that amount be a problem for you?"

She was really asking me to go into business with her; me, the guy who made his living with a lawnmower and a toolbox. The nine hundred and fifty dollars wasn't a problem. I still had a big chunk of my 401k left from the printing company job. And because I was no longer smoking crack and drinking myself into stupidity, most of my hustle money went in the bank.

"No. That wouldn't be a problem at all."

"Are you interested?"

I saw no doubt in her face, and heard none in her words. She believed I could go into business with her. Was I interested? Did I want to be part of her hope, part of her plan, and part of something real? I felt like she was asking me did I want a life again.

I did, and I didn't.

"Why are you bringing this to me, Lena? You probably don't know this, but I had some problems, some serious problems."

I didn't know how much she knew about my past, and I remember thinking obviously she didn't know enough if she wanted to go into business with me.

"I am bringing the idea to you because you are already in the business. And people in the neighborhood like you and trust you. And because you are a business asset."

My life proved me no one's asset. I had destroyed my family and my home life.

"But Lena, I now lost a house, a job, and a wife and family. I was a crack-head for over ten years. I am a fifty-four year old man with a lawnmower and a toolbox. I am not a business asset, I am a loser, and ain't no bank gonna give me anything."

I was looking at her hard, serious, but not mean. I wanted to make

Emotional Drippings

sure she understood what I was saying. She kept her eyes on mine and wrapped her thin fingers around my hand. Her skin, her touch, was soft, warm, and soothing. She put her other hand on our joined hands, and with both of her hands on mine she said, "No person should think of themselves as a loser. I don't think of you as one and neither should you."

And at that moment, with her hands on mine, she sparked something in me. It was the hope of having more. My life consisted of getting up, finding work, and going to bed broke dog tired. That was all I wanted from life, to go sleep exhausted. I needed to be too tired to think because I hated thinking. At night, in my little bed in mama's basement, my thoughts were either about the life I had messed up, or on smoking crack. If I worked myself three leg dog tired, I didn't think, I slept.

"Princeton, the beauty of this business is the minimal start up cost. We won't have to go to a bank to get started. And if we proceed as planned, when it's time to go to a bank we will have the collateral needed. You are not a loser, and please don't ever say that again."

She was looking at me like it was more than me sitting in that chair.

"Listen, I am not the most liked person in the neighborhood. I know what people said and say about me and Mr. Porter. I been hearing their mean spiteful words for years, but I didn't let what people think stop me. And yes . . . I know what people say about you."

I could only guess at what people said about me in the neighborhood. Most of my drug usage was done on the other side of town where my house was at, but people saw me move back home with my mama with no car and no money. They didn't have to be a Sherlock Holmes to figure out my situation. And I know my mama talks.

"But I have watched you Princeton. You kept going despite your set back. All me or anyone else around here sees you doing is working. And that is the type of partner I need. What you did is just that, what you did. It's over.

"People see the good in you. Do you think these old ladies around here would let you in their houses if they didn't see more good in you than bad, and believe me neighbors talk. If you were still doing the things you did that got caused you to lose your home and family, these people around here would know."

My head dropped, but she kept holding my hand.

I wasn't getting high anymore, but I wasn't making real money anymore either. I didn't have a car or hundreds of dollars in my pocket. With those things available to me I might have gotten high again. That was my fear, and that was why I didn't look for another real job. I was too scared.

Getting high had broken me inside, made me unable to trust myself. And even after not using for two years, I still thought about doing it at times. After all the things I lost, the thought of getting high still tempted me, and that scared me more than cancer.

Without looking up at her, I said, "I don't want to let you down."

And I didn't. I was thinking about the thousands of times I told my wife and kids I wouldn't get high and drink again, only to fail. I was remembering being called to the nurse's office at my job for a mandatory employment drug test, and failing. I thought about being in a crack-house and missing my oldest son's college graduation. I thought about my wife crying because I was in the streets missing. People depending on me was not a good thing. I had always let them down.

Lena was offering a life, and I wasn't sure I was ready for one. There

Emotional Drippings

was security in having only a little money, and no car, and no one depending on me.

"You haven't let yourself down, why would you let me down."

"But Lena . . ."

"No buts Princeton. We can do this. I know it. I am willing to take **a** chance on you if you are willing to take a chance on me. I go to work washing out bed pans, and changing pissy, bloody sheets every day. I need something more. We both need this."

I was about to flat out tell her no, but suddenly I started getting poked again in my neck. I hid my first flinch, but more pokes came and the sharp pain forced me to respond.

"Damn!"

I broke free from her hands and grabbed my neck.

"Something is poking me!"

"You feel him?" she asked with her eyes wide, and standing from the kitchen table.

"Hell, yeah, I feel something!"

I stood and swung my arms into the air but touched nothing. More pokes came, and they were getting heavier and harder. They started feeling like stabs. And the kitchen filled with the stink of rotten meat.

"On my God, he's attacking you! You see, he *is* real!"

He was real alright, and he caused me enough pain to fall to the stone tiles of her kitchen floor. On the floor, I felt kicks to my head, gut, back, face, and balls. After the kick to the balls, I got into a knot on the floor. I couldn't see him, but I felt him.

"Mr. Porter please!" I begged.

"Stop it, Mr. Porter! Stop it! He is helping me! You are dead, go where dead people go and leave us alone! I need a man, a living man to

94

help me. Please, Mr. Porter, leave me alone! Leave us alone."

She fell on top of me crying. I un-balled myself underneath her and wrapped my arms around her and rolled on top, trying to cover her against any of his kicks.

"Please, Mr. Porter, please leave us alone," she sobbed.

I tightened up expecting more kicks, but none came. The kitchen lights blinked off and on, cabinet doors slammed, the table rattled, and the china cups and plates flew against the wall shattering. Knives and forks flew from the drawers sticking in walls and the ceiling. I was more than scared if I wasn't lying on top of Lena I would have pissed on myself. The lights stopped blinking and stayed on then all movement in the kitchen stopped, nothing was flying around. Lena was still sobbing and trembling under me.

The stone floor tiles we were laying on were ice cold. The attack stopped. I waited. I felt no more pokes or kicks, and heard only Lena's sobs and breathing. I rolled us both on our sides.

"I think it's over."

I didn't break the hug because she continued to hold on to me. A ghost had kicked my ass, and I was ready to go. But she was still holding me, tight. So I didn't pull away. Mr. Porter had scared her good and me too.

I wanted to make her feel safe, and without really thinking about it, I kissed her. Not sexual like, but supportive like. I kissed her, and then she kissed me.

"Do you think he's gone?" She asked

"I think so." But I didn't know.

I brushed strands of her curly hair from eyes.

"He was really pissed off." She said.

Emotional Drippings

"Yeah, I think so."

I kissed her again, and that time her was mouth open. I felt her warm soft soothing hands on my face and bald head. I felt her heart pounding against my chest.

"Let's get off this cold floor and go upstairs."

She didn't have to tell me twice.

I carried her upstairs to her bedroom and high post bed. Once in the bed she looked at me and smiled. I stood there not sure of what to do. I knew what I wanted to happen, but what I wanted may not have been what she wanted. Then she unsnapped her housecoat and rolled out of it. I hadn't got hard that fast in years.

But thoughts of my ex-wife and family crowded into my head, along with my lost job, my lawnmower, the little bed in my mama's basement, and my fear of using again. Thinking about all that stuff slowed me down. I stood there looking at her nakedness, but not moving.

I told myself she was scared and reacting to the situation, to Mr. Porter haunting her, and she really didn't want me. She needed me to support her, not to fuck her. My instant erection subsided to my thoughts until she stood from the bed and kissed me. My thoughts gave way to what I felt: Lena's soft lips on mine, then on my neck, and her hands sliding into my work pants. Again, I jumped hard immediately.

"Your eyes are telling me yes. Your body is telling me yes," she said while her hand was stoking my hardness, "so why are your clothes still on?"

We laid in her high post bed naked, and kissed ourselves pass doubts and into the possible. The blind-less window was half raised, and the scent of blooming lilacs floating through her bedroom, but there was a hint of something else, that same rotten smell from the kitchen.

With her head on my chest she told me, "You are the man I need."

I had not been what anyone needed once I started smoking crack. And once I got clean, all relationships that I was needed in had been destroyed due to the things I did. To my thinking, no one needed me.

Her words excited a part of me that had died. A man needs to be needed. I took her face into my hands and kissed her soft pouty lips again. All that was in my mind was Lena until my feet turned ice cold then boiling hot. I started to scream but the heat shot through my body.

"Do you know that everything I needed done around here you did? You have proven yourself to me in more ways than you know. And now, you have freed from my dead husband. Do you know how important you are to me?"

I wanted to answer but the heat consumed. I couldn't open my mouth or move at least not by my mind. My head dropped my head to her pretty pair and my tongue began tracing the outline of nipples. It wasn't me doing it, my body was following directions. I was a puppet, a very hot puppet.

"Oh you feel so familiar," she moaned and that was last thing I heard or remembered from our first time.

When I woke up the next morning still in her bed, she was cuddled up on my chest sleep. My knees were stinging when looked down at them I saw carpet burns on both. The tip of my tongue was tender against my teeth and my neck ached. When I looked down at my johnson I almost yelled; it didn't look like mine, it was way longer and thicker even in the soft state, and I was a pretty big fella before. What I saw down there was abnormally large.

I was about to rise from the bed when a voice inside my head said,

Emotional Drippings

"Remain still. Don't wake her up."

And while I was laying there, Mr. Porter, the ghost rises, up out of me. And the motherfucker didn't say a word to me. He just broke up into thousands of little pieces of light and was gone. I immediately looked down to my johnson, but it was back to my normal size. He straight up used me, but he didn't use me up because I got hard from laying naked next to Lena. And since we had already done it, sort of, I nudged her a little with my erection.

She didn't open her eyes but she said, "Again? What are you super man or something? Don't expect too much from me but come on."

She opens her thighs, but not her eyes. I got between her firm thighs, happy. She raised her knees with her thighs open. I put only the head inside her.

With her eyes still closed she said, "Don't play with me, Preston. Put it all in."

And I did. Again and again and again . . .

*

The next Saturday, I didn't mop her kitchen floor. We went to City Hall and registered 'Small Jobs Professionally Done, Inc.' as a small business. Then we rented a room downtown and sealed the deal in a honeymoon suite. Mr. Porter has never returned, and she seldom mentions him, so I think she's happy with me.

My mama says I am being foolish. "She now put one husband in the grave, you next," was her warning. But warning aside, my mother hasn't complained once about the increased rent I been able to pay her by being in business with Lena, or the company truck that allows me to take her to the store and to church.

Lena and I have been in business for sixteen months, and we have remained lovers and best friends. I proposed marriage a couple of months ago, but she said we should wait, and I don't mind because things have been going good following her plans.

The End

Emotional Drippings

The Process

Last year, after her mother died, she stopped believing in God. But this rejection of providence does not stop her from screaming "Sweet Mary Mother of God . . . this damn thing hurts" as she collapses half naked into my director's chair with her left hand cupping her jaw. "That quack gave me Tylenols 3s, but they're not doing a thing for me."

She rocks forward in the chair and her red hair drapes her blue jean covered knees. The yellow flip flops I gave her at the beginning of the semester are on her tiny feet exposing her manicured pink toes. She rocks back in the chair and then forward again. She is topless with her bra dangling from her thumb, and I am trying not to look at her small dancing breasts, but I am looking. Not like I am attracted to them, but I am looking because they are bouncing and circling around as if they could leave her chest if they so desired.

"Damn, this throbbing . . . oh my god . . . if it would stop then I could think." She brings her right hand up to cover her left, and now she has both hands and her bra cupping her jaw.

Sitting across the concrete walled dorm room on my unmade bed, which I made earlier this morning, I am trying to decide if I should go give my best friend a comforting hug or stay seated. My mind is questioning the action because Megan is predictably violent when she is in pain or angry, and she has done much worse than swear *Sweet Mary Mother of God* when hurt or mad.

My eyes move from her to my new black Swiss Army book-bag which is sitting in my lap. I start flipping the zipper with my index finger, and without looking from the zipper I tell her, "I have some Vicodin left from stepping on the nail. You are more than welcome to them." This offer isn't made without consideration. There are only seven Vicodin pills left from the prescription, and I have been using them selectively. The pills have gained value with me.

I stop flipping the book-bag zipper and look up for Megan's answer. My friend's hanging red hair is in a column of morning sunlight. She is moving her head to and fro from naked shoulder to naked shoulder.

She does not stop the swaying her head nor does she raise it to answer me, "No, those pills had me peeing on myself last time."

"Well, that's because you did Tequila shots with them . . . against my advice I might add."

She lifts her head and opens her green eyes with red whites and places them in mine. "Really Francis? Right now you are going to go through a 'I told you so thing' with me. Do you know how fucking bad this tooth hurts? No, of course you don't. You have never had a cavity. You have never had braces. You never had a filling. You have no clue about the pain I am feeling. You know what, yes please . . . go get the freaking pills." She blows an exasperated breath and sits back in the chair extending her little feet and keeps her eyes on me.

I lower my eyes from her evil gaze and remind myself that she is hurting, and that's why she is being a bitch. The pills are in the small pocket of my book-bag, pulling out the pill bottle I toss it over hoping she catches it because I am not going near her.

She lets the pill bottle land at her toes, "What, you carry them around with you?" Not waiting for my answer she picks the pill bottle up, uncaps it, and shakes two into her palm.

Yes, I carry them with me because they make painful moments throughout the day better. Moments like *this* one go a little better with a Vicodin. Now there are only five left in the bottle anyway, and when

Emotional Drippings

they are gone they're gone.

I blow out my own exasperated breath and push my book bag aside and against my better judgment rise up from the twin bed. I bend down to floor and pick up my bottle of spring water and walk my open half emptied bottle of water over to her . . . only because I love her.

She pops the pills on her tongue, takes the bottle and gulps the water, "Thanks. There is no reason for anything to hurt this bad." She lowers her head and exhales again, "When I called my father to tell him about the dentist not taking our insurance, he told me his last tooth ache hurt worse than passing a kidney stone. I laughed, but now I believe him. This whole side of my face hurts, no," she caresses the left side of her face, "this whole side of my head hurts, and I swear the pain is moving down to my neck. I wanted to go to class but walking spreads the pain. I barely made it down the stairs to your room. " She raises her head to see me looking down at her, "Thank you for the pills."

She tries to hand me the water bottle back, nope. I know where Megan's mouth has been, at least some of the places, and I am not drinking behind her. Her fellatio skills have been a topic on this campus since our freshman year. And besides, her tooth ache might be due to an infection which she can keep to herself.

"Take the water."

"No, you keep it. What are you going to do now?"

"Find a dentist when the pain subsides and I can think." She puts the water bottle on the floor and leans back in the chair, closes her eyes, and returns her left hand to cupping her jaw.

With the school dentist not accepting her insurance, she is going to have drive to the city.

"You might have to drive to the city."

"Don't care. I'll drive back home to Dayton if I have to."

"Didn't Dr. Leopold warn you about missing another class?"

"Dr. Leopold will have to understand; if not, fuck him and the whole Biology department."

She is in so much pain, I wonder, "Megan?"

"What?"

"Did you pray?"

Prayer helps me when I am hurting, and I know she is hurting not only from the tooth but from her mom dying as well. We have never talked about it, not before and not after the funeral, and I have tried but she always pushes past the conversation.

"What?" She opens her eyes and slowly sits up in the chair, "Are you deliberately trying to stress me out? I came down her to relax, to get away from my babbling roommate and now you are tripping too. Don't you people understand that I am in fucking pain?"

Perhaps my timing isn't right, and I don't want to upset her, but Jesus does help.

"No. I don't want to upset you. I was just thinking prayer would help."

"Prayer will help huh? I am dealing with real pain here; the delusion of prayer will not help me. Did you pray about being gay?"

"What?"

Damn it, my eye is twitching. I close it halfway to stop the involuntary movement; if she sees it jumping she will know she has upset me and that will fuel her on. She lives for conflict.

"Did you take *that* to Jesus? Did you ask your god to stop you from liking boys?"

Emotional Drippings

"Being gay hasn't caused me any physical pain, and what does my praying have to do with your praying?"

"I'm just saying, if it can help me surely it can help you with your nasty little problem. And what are you talking about no pain? You were in plenty of pain less than a month ago because of being gay."

"What are you talking about? God accepts me as I am Ms. Megan. As he made me, I don't have to pray for him to change me."

I take a deep breath in through my nose so she can't hear me, and I blow it out through my nose as well. I don't want her to know she's getting to me. If she thinks I am calm she will stay calm.

"I don't know about your god accepting you, but I know I did. After you came out, and all your choir and church friends on campus dumped you, it was not you and your god sitting up in here with you making plans to kick all their asses. It was me and you. And it wasn't your god who put on a ski mask with you and shaved Righteous Rachel's head. It was me.

"And you felt better after we did it, didn't you? I know you did because I had to stop you from stomping Rachel's shaved head in. Did you pray then, after you beat her bloody?"

"Shhh, somebody might hear you."

She has me grinning. Yes, it is good to have a violent vengeful ally. I put my hand on her naked shoulder and grip it firmly. She did have to stop me from seriously hurting Rachel. Once I started kicking her I couldn't stop. Whenever I pass her on campus, I still get a strong feeling of satisfaction. Sometimes I go out of my way just to see her. Her hair hasn't grown back yet. She looks like a rude chicken, and I have to bite the inside of my jaw to stop myself from laughing at her.

"Well, if somebody does hear us then pray that your god can get you off, and while you're at it pray for a boyfriend because I think you need to get laid, bad. Now, leave me alone. I came down her to get some rest. My roommate is upstairs crying about her damn hamster dying. And why are you back from class already? Didn't you have a lap?"

She leans back in the chair and closes her eyes. I guess she's done being a bitch for now. My attention goes to a small bundle on the floor in front of the dorm-room desk.

"The TA didn't show up. Is that your t-shirt on the floor?" I point to the bundle.

"Yes, I got real hot in my chest and back so I took it off but then I caught a chill. I'm telling you nothing has ever done me like this before. I was in your bed under the covers and about to fall to sleep when the tooth and my bra started bugging me, so I took the bra off, but the fucking tooth had me cross eyed with pain.

"Are the Vicodin working?"

"Yes, a little, the throbbing has stopped."

I walk over to the desk and pick up her t-shirt and sit in the wobbly chair the school provided.

"Beth loves her pets Megan; you know that. She has had that hamster for two years, so of course she is upset."

Her eyes are still closed but she looks like she's listening.

"It's a rodent. She is crying her eyes out over a pet mouse, and she is 19. Little kids cry over dead hamsters not pre- med majors who dissect small mammals. She was doing all that crying for attention. You should have heard her screaming when I flushed the carcass down the toilet. You would have thought it was a blood relative."

She didn't say that. I must have heard her wrong.

"You flushed it down the toilet?"

Emotional Drippings

"Yes, what else was I to do with it, bury it, pray over it?"

"People grieve differently, Megan. Who are you to deny her the process, her process?"

"Process my ass. She was getting on my damn nerves and making my tooth hurt. I didn't do all that shouting and crying when my mother died, and this girl was crying her eyes out over a ball of fur. It didn't make any sense to me, so yes, I flushed it down the toilet, and I slapped her to calm her hysterics."

No, she didn't.

"You slapped her?"

"I had to, she wouldn't stop screaming."

She is still sitting back in the chair with her eyes closed and speaking very matter of fact.

"After you flushed her hamster down the toilet?"

"I disposed of a rodent carcass."

I put her t-shirt on the desk and sit erect in the chair.

"So, you flushed her hamster down the toilet, slapped her, and left her in the room crying."

"Yes, and came down here to relax, but that doesn't look that it will happen this morning." She opens her eyes and turns her head to face me, "Not with you being all Chatty Cathy."

Understanding is needed here at least for me. So I push on despite her annoyed gaze.

"Why did her crying upset you?"

"Because it was continuous and pointless."

"Pointless?"

"A mouse died."

"It was a loss for her, death."

Now she sits erect, and the look on her face tells me my ten year friend is readying for battle.

"I had a loss, a death and I didn't perform as she is doing. My mother died. My mo – mo – mother died. And I felt no need to bawl like a brainless, emotional, spoiled child. And she shouldn't, either. Fuck her. What gives her the right to cry like that over a mouse, over a fucking mouse . . ."

My best friend slumps forward in the chair and starts trembling from head to toe.

Before I can get to her, she burst out in tears and wails, "My mother is dead and that bitch is crying over a fucking rat. Yes I slapped, I wanted to kill the stupid slut."

When I get to her, I bend down to my friend and hug her as tight as I can and let her cry, sob, and wail. I want to tell her Jesus loves her, but I don't. I hold her tight because *I* love her.

The End

Emotional Drippings

Black Curls

It was a small table for one, but there were two chairs. She saw him looking in her direction, so she made room by holding her paper coffee cup in her hand which allowed him to place his blueberry Danish on the platter-sized table next to her bagel with cream cheese spread.

He sat, and they smiled at each other and agreed the coffee was good enough and the doughnuts and bagels were fresh enough to accept the large crowd in the tight space first thing in the day. She was there most mornings before work, and he was forty-five minutes early for a job interview within his present company. He didn't want to arrive early and look too anxious. She nodded her head understandingly. He watched the black curls in her hair bounce with the nod. She reminded him of someone, but many hours would pass before he remembered who.

Her last bit of bagel took exactly seven chews, and her lips didn't part until she sipped from her coffee cup nearly emptying it. He knew she wasn't going to drain it.

"It was nice meeting you," she said standing and looking into the crowd and not at him.

He smiled and said, "Thanks for sharing your table."

She hoisted her backpack up onto her shoulder and nudged her way through the crowd of office workers. If he were single and younger, he would have stood and cleared a path for her. She was pretty enough to make a young man do things.

His interview went well, and he negotiated for ten percent more than the offer and got it. The workday progressed at a steady pace, and he was on the train ride home when his mind went to the young lady in the coffee shop. The bouncy curls in her hair were just as dark and near black as her eyes. He hoped she didn't think of him as a middle-aged letch for watching her so intently, but he hadn't seen a woman beautiful enough to make him stare in quite awhile.

Mashed potatoes, cabbage, and baked chicken, one of his favorite meals, is what his wife suggested for dinner when he told her about getting the position and the higher salary. Her offices had moved half a mile from their home, but the closer location caused her to work later and cook less, so most nights their dinner came from the deli. "Are you sure you don't want to go out? I have coupons," she said before picking the phone up. He told her the deli was fine.

When she got to her last fork full of mashed potatoes, he watched her chew exactly seven times, and her lips didn't part once. She sipped the last of her wine leaving a small amount on the rim of class. She saw him staring and asked, "What?"

"Oh nothing, I was just remembering when you wore your hair curly."

The End.

Emotional Drippings

The Hotel Helene

"Thomas, to make this thing work you are going have to stay away from old people places and things. You cannot go around your old partying friends, and you cannot frequent the places where you used to party." That was the advice the addictions specialist gave me as I left the seven day inpatient treatment program. I was mandated to the drug treatment program by the court.

Fifty-five days ago I was trickin' off and got caught with three crack rocks and dub of blow in my pocket. My plan that night was to go to this cheap four hour spot called The Hotel Helene on Jackson and Sacramento, but the hooker I was with said she could do whatever needed to be done right there in the car. If the hotel money was included in the money I was to pay her. And the way she popped and licked her lips, made what she said she would do for the hotel money sound so enticing. I had three condoms in my pocket, and the car seats reclined, so I said, "Bet".

We pulled into a dead end alley off of Lake Street. The alley ended at the back of a meat packaging plant and on both sides were tall buildings, seemed like a good spot to me. As soon as I parked and unzipped my jeans, ole girl got busy. I was so into what she was doing that I didn't see the squad car roll up behind us.

It turned out that those cops weren't right. One was Black and the other white, they wouldn't even let me pull up my pants before they snatched me out of my Camry into the dark no longer safe alley. Thinking back, I should have known something was wrong because they didn't have on those flashing blue lights or head lights. Just that little spot light was on.

They made me stand there with my jeans around my ankles while they searched my car. They found the rocks and the blows. The Black cop pulled out a pipe and started smoking my rocks right in front of me. He told me, "this shit is good" and passed the pipe to his partner who put another one of my rocks on the pipe and smoked it, and me with my pants still around my ankles.

Then the black cop takes the hooker to the backseat of their squad car, and I see her head disappear. The white cop tells me to pull my pants up, then cuffs me while he's holding a hot crack pipe in his hand. He put more of my dope on the pipe and kept smoking. When the Black cop got out of the squad car the white cop replaced him in the backseat. The Black cop walked up on me and said "You know you going to jail right?" and hits me in the stomach. For services rendered, they let the hooker go, but they did take me to jail and charged me for the dub of blow.

I was held for two weeks, but the truth be told, I got off easy with the mandated drug treatment program. There were a lot brothers in the lock up that was going away for some serious time because of a couple of blows and rocks. But since that was my first time being arrested for possession, I was mandated to an inpatient program for heroin addicts.

I did learn some stuff during those seven days. I learned that I do have the disease of addiction, and that I am addict. Since I had never had heroin withdrawal sickness from the blows, a guy like me didn't think he was addict. I knew I smoked too much crack, but I didn't think I was an addict. A brother was misinformed, but the facts are the facts and they speak for themselves. My past behavior proved me to be an addict.

I have a decent a job for a twenty-three year old, a real decent job. I make more money than my father, got the position by answering one

Emotional Drippings

of those corny ads in the newspaper. It read, 'Do you want to get rich?' It turned out to be telephone sales job, and from the start I did well.

When the trainer told us we could easily make fifty thousand dollars a year, I believed him. I wanted to be a success at the job because it was one of the few things a brother could do that paid well that didn't revolve around a leg. With only a high-school diploma, my options for gainful employment were slim in the city of Chicago.

This week my check is thirteen hundred dollars. I'm back to earning the type of money I was making before jail and the mandated treatment. A brother was clocking thirteen to fifteen hundred dollars a week for three months straight. And I smoked up everything, but my car note money and my rent money.

The truth be told though, the last three checks before I got busted, everything got smoked up. Car note and rent money got smoked up too, and I was starting to miss work on a regular basis.

The guy who trained me was the same person who started me smoking rocks. While I was locked down, he overdosed and had a heart attack and died. And the truth be told, I'm glad he's dead. I wouldn't introduce a dog to smoking crack, never mind a young cat.

The trainer played me good. He appealed to my obvious weakness. He asked me had I ever got my johnson and balls sucked at the same time. When he asked me that question I was still a virgin. A nineteen-year-old, Black male virgin, I'd never had anything sucked.

And it was no mystery to me as to the cause of my virginity. When girls see me, all they see is my plastic leg and thick glasses. My uncle tried to buy me a woman once, but when she called me a 'poor little one legged boy,' I changed my mind and left. Pity has always pissed me off.

The girls the trainer took me to didn't even notice my leg. At least they acted like they didn't notice it. All they noticed was how many rocks we brought. I started out going with him to The Hotel Helene only on big paydays, but then the trainer moved into the hotel, but the next thing a guy like me knew, I was over his place every payday.

Sex and crack was a wicked combination for a virgin boy of nineteen. It didn't take long for me to come up with the idea that I should move to the neighborhood where the hotel was, not in the hotel but close. Five blocks away proved to be far enough away to stop my immediate degradation.

The money that would have rented me a one-bedroom apartment in my parents neighborhood, rented me a whole house in the area of the hotel. Pretty soon I had three women living with me. Of course none of them paid me any rent or brought any food, but they did have rocks when I didn't. I got paid on Fridays, but I was usually smoked out by the following Tuesday. They managed to get me two or three rocks a day until Friday. When Friday came, I bought plenty for all.

When I came home one Tuesday, all three girls were gone along with my two televisions, all my clothes, the microwave, my new stereo, the kitchen table and chairs, the security screen doors, and the bedroom set my mother gave me.

I changed the locks, and never let anybody else move in again. Besides, when I had rocks there was always a new woman or two around to smoke them with, and they usually weren't shy about spending the night. So plenty of mornings I woke up and rolled into a different woman.

The truth be told, a brother does miss the women. But I don't miss being dead broke, hungry, depressed, and damn near homeless . . .

Emotional Drippings

which is where over three years of smoking crack had me. Before my addiction was full blown a guy like me had plenty of fun with the women. I don't have fun like that now. I go to work, to the meetings and back here. My life kind of went back to how it was before I started smoking crack.

I never had one girl friend in high school, not one. Never went on a date, and never got a girl's real phone number. None of the girls in high school or from my block ever really noticed me. All they saw was my plastic leg and thick glasses. I started smoking crack and actually had sex with two of the finest girls that went to my old high school class. True, they weren't as fine as they were in high school, but I still had them.

After the mandated treatment was over, I came back here to my house by the Hotel Helene. The first thing I did was tell the neighborhood rock boys that I wasn't getting high anymore. I had to do this because they were in the habit of stopping by here and asking me if I was 'straight'. After the three girls that lived with me left, the rock boys in the neighborhood began to extend me credit until payday. I would owe each one close to a hundred dollars every Friday.

A couple of them actually offered me credit after I told them I quit. The rock boys in my area are very competitive. The second day I was out one of the three girls who had lived with me before came over with a couple of rocks, but I told her she had to smoke them somewhere else. I guess she told everyone else because no one knocks on my door anymore.

I'm thinking about moving back in with my parents because the main reason I moved here was to get high. And since a brother is no longer getting high, living here doesn't make any sense. I been going to the meetings like the addictions specialist suggested. But I haven't found a sponsor yet, nor have I found a meeting where I really feel comfortable.

All the people at the meetings I go to are way older than me, and it seems like they all been getting high for twenty years and have pretty much fucked up their lives. Hardly any of them work, and they all be begging me for my squares. Next week I'm going to try some meetings on the other side of the city and see what's up with them.

Today is my fifty-fourth day clean and the truth be told, I feel really good, except for one thing . . . a brother is way too horny. I haven't had any since the night I got caught with the hooker, and I really didn't get to finish then. A guy like me is way overdue for some.

I haven't been up to The Hotel Helene since I got clean because of what the addictions specialist told me. But I can't think of a better place to take care of this type of need. At the hotel I'll have a choice of ladies to choose from, and besides, a brother got paid today. I might get me a couple of girls, a little reward for being clean.

*

Pulling up in front of the hotel, I feel the same type of rush I got when I was coming here to cop rocks. My heart is beating just as fast, and I can barely wait to get in there. Damn. I don't like this feeling, but it's all good though because I didn't come here to buy any crack. A brother is just stopping by to get a couple of females.

"Thomas! Well look at you! Darling you are looking wonderful. You don't have to tell me I can look at you and see it! You now left that stuff alone! Come on around here and hug me! Baby I'm so proud of you."

Mattie is probably the sweetest woman in the world next to my

Emotional Drippings

mother. And I truly care about her, and I missed her. But like many old people, places, and things in my life, I had to stay away from her. I got plenty high at this hotel, and this is the only place I knew to come see her, so a brother didn't see her.

"Hey, Mattie!"

"Boy, you better get on around here and hug my neck!"

She buzzes me in from the small entrance lobby into the larger lobby of the hotel. Mattie comes from behind the security glass and gives me a big hug.

"Thomas I am so happy for you!" When we break loose from the hug, I see her eyes are watering. "I prayed for you. I knew God had you some place safe."

I start the second hug. I lean into the mass of Mattie and remember how she ran me up out of the hotel the last time I was here.

I'd been getting high for three days and would have continued until every dime I had in my pocket was spent. Last year my tax refund was over twenty five hundred dollars. I told myself and the babe I was with that only five hundred dollars was going to be spent on crack.

There was less than two hundred dollars in my pocket when Mattie came into my room with a bucket of hot water and a broom. She ran me out of the hotel in my BVDs. She threw me out my pants and locked the doors on me. I saw her standing behind the glass door crying.

In her ear I whisper, "Thank you, Mattie. You saved my life that day."

And when I look back on it, she probably did. She made me stop for a while, thus giving my heart a much needed break, but once I got back home I spent the rest of my money with the neighborhood rock boys.

"No baby... Jesus saved your life. He told me to run you out of that room. Come on, let's go over here and sit for a minute. I want you to catch me up. You look good, being drug free agrees with you."

We walk across the poorly lit lobby to a sagging forest green velvet sofa. It's a bright day outside but none of the sun's cheer has made its way inside the hotel lobby. Mattie rest her heavy frame, she and the sofa sigh.

"So how long you been clean?"

Sitting next to her I answer, "fifty-four days."

"Mmmph, mmph, mmph, now you know that's the Lord and it looks like He been having His way with you every since."

Neither of us say anything but it's not awkward. I am in the presence of an elder who cares about me. Her warmth surrounds me. When I look at her, a guy like me can tell she's proud of a brother and that she is truly happy for me.

"Not a day went by that I didn't think about you." She grabs a hold of my hand. "You never belonged around here Thomas, at least not getting high. You are smart enough to do something for this community, not be part of the problem. It hurt me, seeing all that good inside you going to waste." I smell Mattie's floral perfume, and another all too familiar scent.

"I have never been all that good, Mattie."

"You have a good heart. There is a lot of love inside you. You care for people. Every crack head and dope-fiend around here knew all they had to do was tell you a sob story and you would give them some of what you had."

"Yeah, I guess that is true."

Emotional Drippings

She pulls me into another embrace.

"I hope you didn't come here to get none of that mess. You looking good now. You should never go back to using that stuff." She says into my ear. When she releases me she looks beyond my face and to my heart she says, "Seeing you like that, all cracked out and burnt up, hurt. It not only hurt me but other people in the neighborhood too. Folks notice you Thomas. You are the topic of conversation at least once a week in this lobby. People guessing about what happened to, 'the little one leg fella'. A lot of people around here care about your narrow behind." She points to the mirrored wall across the lobby. "Look at yourself, see how good you look drug free."

I see both of our reflections in the mirror. Mattie has on her flowered satin finish purple moo moo, and I am in a white oxford button down shirt with a pair of dress black slacks and polished ox blood penny loafers. I do look good even with the black horn rimmed glasses.

Mattie anchors her left hand on the arm of the sofa and pushes herself up. She tells me to remain seated. She goes into the reception area and returns with a photograph. It's a picture of me and Beth, one of the girls I use to kick it with, and we're both 'tore up from the floor up'. I couldn't have weighed a hundred and thirty pounds. On my head is a beat-up black base-ball cap, my jeans were creased but dirty and my shirt was an old Chicago Bears t-shirt. I remember taking this picture, me and Beth were off to the movies. We were going to do something besides getting high that night.

"Beth still stays here off and on. She hasn't changed much from when you two took the picture. Maybe she's a little thinner."

Beth and I are the same height, five feet seven inches. She couldn't have weighed a hundred pounds at the time of the photo.

"When was the last time you saw her Mattie?"

"This morning, she's upstairs now." She wipes her hand backwards over her short graying afro. Mattie's looking at me hard. I had never noticed the two little moles over her right eye before. Her brown eyes cast down then back to mine. "I don't think you should see her. She'll pull you down before you bring her up."

She thinks I have come to the hotel looking specifically for Beth, she's wrong.

"Mattie I didn't come here just looking for her. I mean I would like to see Beth, but Jasmine, Renee, or even Brenda would make me happy."

"Oh!" She smiles a big smile that opens up her whole round face. "Now I see, you didn't stop by here just to hug my neck. They say that when you put the stuff down your nature comes back stronger." She slaps me on my thigh. " Well I understand baby, as long as it ain't that stuff . . . you know, it's a new girl been staying here and she don't get high, I been sending a couple of nice young men up to see her. I'ma call her down for you to see."

"You say she don't get high?"

"Not to my knowledge, let me call her room."

The desk buzzer sounds, Mattie has customers.

"Hold on Thomas, be right back."

For a heavy elderly woman she moves well, she's up and at the glass before I could stand. One of the first nights I stayed at the hotel I experienced how fast she was personally.

I tried to sneak out the back door because I went two hours past check out time and had smoked up all my money. I was a good five

Emotional Drippings

steps ahead when she saw me at the back door. Before I could push the bar on the door she had me by the collar.

I offered her my watch for collateral. She laughed at it and told me a man is only as good as his word. She released my collar when I promised to pay her. I brought her the money the next morning and we've been friends every since.

In the hotel outer lobby is a very tall man in a green khaki uniform. With him is a tiny woman in a thin plum dress. She has on white deck shoes and her callused heels are on the backs of them. She's pulled her hair together in a nub of a pony tail held together by a blue rubber band. Judging by her nervous continuous smile, her anxious hip twisting, her foot patting and her consistent rubbing of the Tall man's shoulder; he has already brought what she wants.

He doesn't look like the type that gets high every day, she does. Little does he know that when they get to the room, her desire will be taken care of before his. And if he's as new to the game as he looks, her desire will become his. The only thing that will happen in that room will be the smoking of cocaine.

I began visualizing the tiny woman upstairs in a room with her crack pipe and lighter in hand. This is not a healthy thought for me, but it is a comfortable thought. I can clearly see her taking a hit and exhaling large clouds of crack smoke. Part of my mind tells me to move past this thought, but I don't. I linger in the thought of smoking cocaine.

Watching the tiny woman in the lobby twisting in expectation, I become very conscious of the thirteen hundred dollars in my pocket. As my toes began to curl and my butt tightens, my mind wanders to the room on the third floor. It is the last room on the left. In the room, a hundred fifty dollars could buy me an eight ball of cooked cocaine.

Crack.

The aroma of smoked crack from the upstairs rooms went barely noticed earlier, now the scent fills my head. I shake my head hard, trying to clear the rising desire. The elevator door to the right of Mattie's office area opens. The woman on it is wearing a pink and black housecoat and it's open at the top, exposing her breast. She has long nipples. Our eyes meet, hers are bucked wide open. She's high. She smiles and beckons me.

The door from the outer lobby opens. The big man and tiny woman walk past me and get on the elevator. The woman stays on the car with the big man and the tiny woman.

"Bitch close your clothes, he's with me." The tiny woman says to the buck eyed one, standing in front of the big man. The elevator door closes. They're gone, but I want to shoot up the stairs behind them. I haven't seen breast in the flesh for close to two months. So what if she was high, she had her titties out.

I stand up ready and notice the light panel above the elevator stopped at two. I walk across the lobby and push the elevator button. Mattie has more customers at the desk. The right thing to do would be tell her I was going upstairs, but the elevator door opens, and Ms. Long Nipples with her titties out is still on the car. I step in and without hesitation I cup her right breast and began licking her nipple.

"Oh-wee, let's go, baby. I'm in room 305."

We go from the elevator to her room, and her nipple is still in my mouth. I stop sucking when I hear her close the door behind us. It's a small room with a big bed. I reach into my pocket to pay her. I know I can get what I want for twenty. But because I don't want to be rushed and I want her happy and surprised, I peel off a fifty and hand to her.

Emotional Drippings

"Oh yes baby, Randi is going to take care of you fo' real now!"

She slides the fifty under the lamp on her bedside table and says, "When what I do starts feeling good to you, I want you to call my name. And call it loud!"

Randi steps out her robe completely, her body is thin but not bony. She has curves and a nice firm booty which I grab a hold of. She unbuckles my belt, opens my pants and unzips my fly. She puts her hand in my BVDs and wraps her fingers around me.

"Oh yes baby, I'm glad you thick and ready! It's been awhile since I had a fat one. Pull them pants on off."

Now this is where I get nervous. Taking off my pants and revealing my prosthesis is a problem for me, particularly when I'm sober. When I got high it wasn't a problem because then me and the girls were mostly concerned about the crack, not my leg. Getting naked was just a step in the process. The real event was getting high.

But now that I am not high, there is a real concern as to how she will view me. My leg below my right knee is the prosthesis. I wasn't born with that part of my leg, or a baby toe on my left foot. She is moving too fast for me to offer an explanation or objection. Before I know it my pants are down around my ankles.

I step out of them and pick them up from the floor. I feel for my wallet and cash, they are still in the pockets. I lay my pants across her bed and I sit on them. She pulls off my BVDs and puts her head between my legs.

She's got skills and I am responding to them. I need this here. A brother is close to doing what is expected when she suddenly grabs a hold of my johnson tight and says, "No, no, no! I gots to ride this pony."

When she mounts, she takes it all in easily and rides. It's wet and loose, but she knows how to go from sloppy to snug and rides from tip to base. I'm about to pop off but she raises all the way up off me and drops back down on me with a tighter, dryer grip, this is not the same orifice. I explode.

"You forgot to call my name," she says. When I open my eyes she's smiling down at me. "I told you to call my name." She rolls off of me and I close my eyes again. I ain't moving a muscle cause brother is too spent to twitch.

I hear a lighter click, followed by the sizzle of a lit a crack rock.

Everything I learned in treatment and everything I heard at the meetings lets me know that it's time to leave. I don't open my eyes but I feel her moving towards me. She is blowing the warm smoke on my nipple. The inviting vapor flirts under my nose. Her tongue which is going down my stomach distracts me from the scent of the crack. She is between my legs. Now she has her tongue in an area that was previously only touched while cleaning. She stops, and again I hear the click and the sizzle.

"Put your knees up baby."

I open my eyes briefly and watch her adjust my legs to how she wants them. She grabbed a hold of my prosthesis as if it was a leg. I close my eyes when she lights her pipe again. She's blowing smoke in that same private area.

Now she's licking all up in that area. And this is way more than I can take. I try to squirm free but she grabs me by the waist and keeps on licking me there. I'm only half hard but I'm spurting all over myself. She has my whole body wired, everywhere she touches cause me to tremor. She's only rubbing my knees but it feels erotic. She's up at my

Emotional Drippings

chest and she's licking my nipples again.

"What I got to do to make you scream my name?"

"Randi," I say.

"Louder!"

"Randi!" I yell.

The bathroom door is kicked open from the inside, and out comes this big dude with a cocked pistol.

"You know what this is! Now toss me them clothes you laying on," he directs.

I don't even hesitate, they got me. Randi jumps out the bed and gets back into her housecoat. She buttons it all the way up and slides into some jeans. The big sucker with a half braided head is going through my pockets and he's counting my cash like it's his. I guess it is now. He opens up my wallet and smiles at the credit cards. He puts the cash in my wallet and drops it into a pillowcase with all my clothes and my shoes.

The big guy tells Randi, "Take his leg."

"Huh?" Randi and I say at the same time.

"I said take his damn leg. I know a place where we can pawn it." She doesn't hesitate to un-strap my prosthesis.

"Don't even think about coming out of this room." The wild-haired big guy says slamming the door behind them.

They took my money, my clothes, and my leg. They left me buck naked and scared.

*****

This is messed up. I've been laying here for over thirty minutes uncertain of what to do next. My only choice is to wrap myself in a sheet and call down to Mattie. This is really messed up. I turn my head and look at the lamp on the bedside table. I don't think it's there but I look under it anyway, and it is there, the fifty-dollar bill I gave Randi. She also forgot four rocks, a lighter, and an antennae pipe. I'll be damn.

Without a second thought I stuff a rock in the end of the pipe and start to light it when I hear, "Thomas! Are you in there baby?"

Mattie is banging on the door. She opens it before I can wrap up in the sheet, but I do drop the pipe and lighter. She comes in with my leg and clothes in tow.

"Baby, are you okay?"

"You got my stuff!"

"Yes, my security caught they no good asses trying slip out the back. If they would have paid their bill, they would have got away. You lucky they trifling, here you go." She puts my stuff on the foot of the bed. I strap on my prosthesis.

Not looking directly at me she says, "You go on and get dressed. Then come on downstairs. I'm going to let them go because I don't want the police coming all up in here. If you want to slap them or something, come on down while my security got hold of them. Are you okay, baby?"

I open my wallet and see all my cash and credit cards.

"I'm better than okay, Mattie." I stand up to give her a hug forgetting my nakedness.

She jumps back, "Boy you better put on your clothes. I'll see you when you get down stairs." She turns for the door, "You shoulda waited for the nice girl I had in mind for you. You lucky that trifling ass Randi didn't have you high up in here!" She pulls the door up and leaves.

When she says that I look down at the pipe and lighter which are

125

Emotional Drippings

barely under the bed. I bend down to pick them up. I need a hit after all this. It won't hurt anybody. I'll just start over with the meetings and stuff.

I light the lighter and there is a soft tap at the door. Beth walks in, skinny, raggedy, and nasty. I can smell her musk from the doorway.

"I heard you was up here Thomas. What's that you got there?" The pipe and lighter are in my hand. Her eyes go to the rocks on the bedside table. "Awright now baby, it's gonna be like old times!"

Hearing her say, 'It's going to be like old times,' is reality slapping me in the face. Instantly, I drop the pipe and the lighter. Looking at Beth, I don't see her; I see myself, a using, non-washing, no hope for the future self. I hurriedly get dressed as Beth gathers up the remaining rocks, "Come on baby. We can go up to my room."

I hear her. My response is, "I got to go, Beth. I don't want to get high again. I can't."

She has a confused look on her face, but I can't stay to explain. A brother gots to go. I give Mattie a wave goodbye and limp my stupid grateful ass up out of the Hotel Helene.

The End

A Day and a Chance

He slung the free end of the vinyl laundry line over the copper cold
water pipe. The only light in the basement of the abandoned two flat
brick building was the flickering flame of his candle. He watched his
shadow wavering on the water damaged gray concrete blocks. The
basement walls, the furnace, and a few pipes were the only solid
structures remaining.

The building had been condemned three years ago. It was his
grandfather's first building, but no one cared that his grandfather once
owned the place. He, his grandfather, and the rest of his family were no
longer a part of the neighborhood. He considered the building and the
women he brought there the same, things no one cared about.

Wood chips, dust, and bits of dried insects fell from the old pipe
into his eyes as he adjusted the laundry line. He blinked the debris from
his eyes. The woman on the other end of the line was like all the
others, skin and bones. He hoisted her as easy as a sack of potatoes. He
tied the free-end of the line to the metal base of the ancient furnace
that once warmed his family. She swung upside-down from the
coldwater pipe. She was gagged and bound with silver duct tape. He
kicked her in the head with the side of his hiking boot, adding
momentum to her swing.

He stood behind her naked hanging body and slapped her small bare
buttocks. The dose of Valium was only to relax her, not render her
unconscious. There was no water and he didn't want to waste his beer
splashing her in the face. He simply had to wait, but waiting was no
problem. It was Friday night, the beginning of the weekend. He blew
out the candle and laid down on the floor beneath her swinging head,
listening to her rapid breathing. When her breathing changed, the party

Emotional Drippings

would begin.

****

Patrice felt his hands on her face. She felt the moisture of his breath, and she felt the line cutting into her ankles. She smelled the candle and the dampness of the basement. All she could think to do was pray and hope that God would give her another chance.

****

Samuel Davis parked his bronze '85 Buick Regal in the White Castle's parking lot on 35th and King Drive facing the bus stop. It was the end of another double shift day at the bakery. He was still dressed in his sanitary whites and work boots. The smell of the bakery claimed the car.

Samuel loved the smell. The scent represented legitimate work, something he thought he'd never have. Good jobs were hard to find in Chicago. The better paying jobs were in the suburbs. He was fortunate and he knew it. Checking the clock in the dashboard it read five forty-five p.m. Patrice was late.

He tried to push aside the feelings of doubt that were entering his mind. A year ago he wouldn't have waited ten minutes for her, he would have simply left. This year she wasn't the same woman, and he wasn't the same man. Over the past year they had built something; they had an apartment, a car, and had gotten both of their kids back from State-care. They were a family, a family of which they both were proud of. But if she didn't hurry up, he would have to leave and come back for her.

After six p.m. the day care charged twenty dollars for every fifteen minutes late. Since the state was no longer paying the bill, he had to be on time. Good job or not, twenty dollars for fifteen minutes was more

128

than his family could afford.

****

His eyes had become accustomed to the dark. He gripped her head with calloused hands and thumbed her eyes opened. She was awake. Her alert eyes darted from side to side with fear. Anger took him. How did he let this ignorant cockroach of a woman deny him minutes of pleasure? He slapped her face hard and rose from beneath her swinging head.

The basement would be completely black to her. Knowing that brought a tight grin to his pitted face. He grabbed her by her narrow hips, stopping her slight swaying. He held her nude body completely still, bent his head to her buttocks and bit into her left cheek. His nicotine stained teeth sank into her skin. She whimpered, squirmed and tried to twist free. He held her in place and pressed his teeth down until he tasted blood. He thought about biting out a chunk of her butt, but stopped tearing into her when he remembered the last time he bit a piece of flesh from one of these worthless women. The woman passed out, and he had to wait almost an hour for her to wake up.

He heard this one whimpering, and the sounds pleased him. Her muffled crying excited him to an erection. Her quiet sobs were like promises of agonizing the moans and groans to come. Ones that whimpered in the beginning, wept and pleaded in the end. He needed more light to really get started. He bent to the floor and fumbled around for the box of candles. He wanted a new one, a long one. With candle in hand, he took his square metal flip top lighter from his soiled pants pocket. He pulled her body against his own anchoring her into position. He forced the candle down into her. When he was satisfied that it was in deep enough to stand alone and steady, he released her

129

Emotional Drippings

and lit the wick.

****

Samuel parked in front of the day-care on 35th and Giles. When he walked in Tasha was sitting patiently waiting in a small chair by the door. She had on a yellow Looney Tunes coat with a matching Tweety Bird hat, and her multi-colored Looney Tunes book bag was in her lap.

Patrice's bright eyes and smile greeted him from their daughter's chubby face. Being worried about Patrice didn't stop Samuel from returning his daughter Tasha's smile. She hopped up with excitement and ran to greet him with an embrace only his daughter could give him, a hug that gave purpose to his life. Kenny, the boy child of the family was not waiting patiently. He was running through the day-care as if he was in a group of ten kids, and was making enough noise to equal all ten.

Kenny didn't have on his coat or his hat, and his gym shoes were untied. Ms. Newman, the owner of the center, looked exhausted. She ignored Kenny's disturbance and glanced up at the center's big Pooh Bear clock, Samuel had three minutes to spare. He smiled at her, and she shook her head smiling slightly. She was a nice lady, but she strictly enforced the late charges. They were both relieved that she didn't have to penalize Samuel.

Kenny saw his father but he was determined to make one more round of the day-care before he left. Samuel blocked his path and scooped him up. He tried to squirm free but Samuel held him firm and tickled him in the ribs. He squealed in mischievous joy and gave in to his father.

With his children strapped into their car seats and chattering about the day-care Samuel drove back to the bus stop hoping and praying that Patrice would be waiting. He pulled into the same spot in the White Castle parking lot facing the bus stop, no Patrice. Daylight savings time had begun last week, the city was dark at six. The night made Patrice tardiness more apparent.

"Where is Mommy, Daddy?" Tasha asked.

"She had to work a little later baby?"

"But she's coming home tonight right?" Kenny asked.

"You will see her before you go to sleep."

After another twenty minutes clicked off the Buick's clock, he pulled the cell phone from the glove compartment and dialed the nursing home where Patrice worked, and was told she wasn't there. He put the cell phone back in the glove compartment and started the car. When he looked in the rearview mirror his eyes met Tasha's. She was only four but she seemed to sense when things were wrong. He smiled at her in the mirror and told both his children they were going over Big Mama's for a little while. Kenny yelled in happiness. Tasha looked out the window into the night.

****

What kind of crazy bastard was he? Did he plan to kill her? Sweet Jesus why did she stop for him? She had more than enough money to buy her own crack-rocks. She'd seen him before with other girls. They all talked about how much money he spent, and how good he ate pussy. He was supposed to be safe. Why was he doing this to her? She didn't deserve to die like this, hung upside down like a pig about to be gutted.

Seven times worse is what the old timers at the meetings told her. If she went back out to the streets and got high, it would be seven times worse. She thought she had proved them wrong, because the first

Emotional Drippings

couple of times she'd gotten high with no problems.

When she got off of work early, she rode the bus down a couple of stops past her normal stop, met one of the young rock selling boys walking and bought a couple of rocks. She went home and smoked them. Nobody knew, and no one got hurt. She had been sneaking successfully.

She would still be getting high that way if it had not been for the lay off. She wanted to get real high today, and the white man was known to get real high with girls. It was suppose to be so simple, get him off and get high. This mess wasn't part of her plan. She thought he was a normal trick, not some psycho. Seven times worse, and they were right. This crazy bastard was seven times worse than anything she'd experienced in the past.

****

Samuel didn't spend a minute in his house. He went in, saw Patrice wasn't there and left. His explanation to his mother was brief, Patrice was missing and he had to go find her. He kissed her and his children goodbye and began his search.

He knew where to start, the strip. Patrice was no different than other people that slipped back into getting high. They went to familiar places, and the strip was common ground for them both. He knew she had relapsed. No other explanation would take root in his mind.

He drove down 47th Street checking both sides of the street. He saw faces he knew, but he did not want to ask them had they seen his wife. His wife, the mother of his children, the woman he was planning a new and better life with. No, he wasn't going to ask anyone had they seen her. He would simply find her.

He drove by four or five dope spots and saw no signs of her. The next step was to go into a couple of crack-houses. People would be surprised to see him. Some would be happy, hoping he was back to smoking rocks and had some money. They would be disappointed. He was going to go in and out. If Patrice was not there, he would leave and go to another crack-house. He hadn't set foot in a smoke--house in over eighteen months. He was well warned against old people places and things. More than one recovering addict had fallen because of past associations. He parked his car on 47th and King Drive and began his walk.

****

He had lit more candles; over thirty burned in the basement. He was satisfied. It was enough light to watch the worthless woman flinch with each hot drop of wax that dripped on her back. He could see her pleading eyes filled with tears. He thought about cutting her down to give her some false hope, but decided against it. He pulled his snub-nose wire cutters from his back pocket, and gripped her baby toenail with it. He asked her had she ever had a pedicure, and yanked the nail from her toe. The blood didn't gush as he hoped, it leaked. He drew the candle that he forced into her free, and dripped wax on the injured toe. He asked, "Was that better"?

He looked into her eyes and saw them fading. He didn't want her to pass out. He stripped the duct tape from her mouth, allowing her to gasp for air.

****

Patrice's first thought was to scream for help. She quickly put the thought aside, thinking that screaming might anger him. She wasn't sure what he'd done to her foot. She felt some slight pain, but both her feet were numb from the clothes line. She was sure her back was blistered.

Emotional Drippings

It had to be because the candle wax drops burned so. Maybe if she begged him and promised him anything, he would let her go.

Her own voice sounded foreign to her ears. It was raspy and barely above a whisper. She wanted to speak louder, but the volume wasn't there. He must have heard her because he pulled up a plastic milk crate and sat in front of her. She asked, "Please cut me down."

She begged him to cut her down. She told him she couldn't do the things he asked her to do earlier, tied up like she was. She heard his zipper come down. He put his hand on the back of her neck and pulled her head into his lap. In his other hand he held a butcher knife. She felt the tip pressing into the base of her neck. He ordered her to, "Make me bust a nut." If he came he promised to cut her down.

*****

Samuel heard and felt his own heart beating as he walked up the stairs. Crack-houses were a thing of the past for him. They had no purpose in his present life and he had no business being at one, this he knew. He had eight hundred and twenty five dollars cash in his pocket. Today was payday. He and Patrice enjoyed grocery shopping and paying bills together. There was a time they didn't do either. A time when both of them were stuck in a crack-house, smoking up grocery and rent money. Now he had both in his pocket, grocery and rent money, and he was standing at the door of a crack-house. He raised his hand to knock, but he dropped it. He couldn't risk it. He couldn't risk going into a crack-house even for Patrice. The life he had now, was better than the life he and Patrice had eighteen months ago. This life he respected, he earned it. And Patrice should respect it as well. They both had too much to lose, and if she didn't know it, he knew it.

Patrice was a grown woman who knew what he knew about staying drug free. Yes he loved her, but he also loved Tasha, and Kenny. They depended on him. Patrice was doing wrong, he had to do right. He turned his back on the door, and went down the steps taking two at a time.

The word coward entered his mind as he started the Regal. He laughed. Yes, he was a coward where crack-rocks are concerned. They had beaten him enough. He knew he had no strength against them. His best weapon against the drug was to stay away from it. He had a family to protect. Yes Patrice was part of his family, but she was in an area where he could not and would not tread. She was on her own.

****

Patrice fell to the basement floor hard. He cut her loose after he released in her face. She twisted her hands free of the tape, and wiped his filth from her face. She tried to stand up, but her feet and knees were too weak. She raised herself up, and got into a crawling position. He was behind her. She felt one of his hands on her back. The other held her hip. He was still hard, she felt him forcing himself inside her. She knelt on the dirt floor, and let him finish his business. If he satisfied himself, he might let her go, was her thought. She heard his grunt of completion, but he remained inside her.

She told him, "That was good Daddy." And squirmed a little for his pleasure, "That was the first time I came in months. Maybe, there is something to being tied up and spanked."

She heard him chuckle as he rolled off of her. She didn't try to get up. She rolled towards him instead, and cuddled against him. She asked him, "Where did you learn this game?"

He didn't answer. He sat up and cut her feet free of the laundry rope.

Emotional Drippings

Patrice saw stairs leading up on the far side of the basement, but she didn't see a door. Maybe in the darkness of the other side of the basement a door existed. She put her thoughts on what she could see, the stairs. He stood up. He was a big man, four times her size. He went to a duffle bag and pulled out a blanket. He spread it on the floor and ordered her to it.

She smiled at him and crawled to the blanket. The blanket was closer to the stairs. She sat and watched him fumble through his pockets. He pulled out a plastic lighter, a metal crack pipe, and a hand full of cocaine rocks. He tossed the items to her and grinned.

****

She delayed his true pleasure. This worthless woman made him have a climax. So there was a temporary delay from the ecstasy of watching her die. He always came then. He rewarded her with the only thing any of them really cared about, those damn crack rocks. It had been over two years since he reached an orgasm through sex with a living woman. Their dead bodies proved much more permitting. No waiting for them to smoke another rock. No complaints about anal sex. Dead bodies bent to his will.

Never in his life had a woman told him he gave her an orgasm without oral sex. There was always a complaint about his limited duration. She said she came. Well, that got her a couple of more moments of agony free life, and one last good high. What was it she asked him, where did he learn this game. Did she really think it was a game? Well if so, the end would definitely be a surprise to her.

****

Patrice didn't want to get high. She wanted to get him talking, and hopefully get his mind off of her death. She knew he did not plan to let her leave. Killing her would be the only way to stop her from going to the police. She had to convince him that she was not a threat. That she enjoyed his game and would like to play it another day. To do that, she had to get him talking. She patted the spot on the blanket and asked, "Why don't you come closer and sit next me?"

He took his clothes off, and came to her with butcher knife in hand.

"Why do you need the knife," she asked trying to look him in the face despite the poor light of the candles.

"To cut your heart out after we are finished," he answered.

She giggled and patted him on the chest, "You play the game so well, keeping me scared and turned on at the same time. It's exciting."

She offered him the pipe. He refused and ordered her to smoke a rock.

She thought about what some of the other girls had told her about him. He liked to go down on women. She sat facing him with her knees up and her thighs open. After she melted a rock on the antennae pipe, she opened the lips of her vagina and fingered herself for him to watch. No man who liked oral sex could watch a woman playing with herself without wanting to taste, at least not in her experience.

She moaned and twisted in pseudo pleasure while she inhaled the smoke from the crack-rock. She saw the corners of his mouth raise in a smile. She watched his tongue lick his thin lips. She circled her opening with her forefinger, and she increased her moans. She watched him watching her intently through the candle light. She thumbed her clitoris, and gasped in the phony pleasure. She begged him for his assistance.

"All I need is a little lick right here, just a little one, right on the tip of my pearl tongue. Can you do that for me Daddy? Right here on the

Emotional Drippings

tip. I'll come again if you do that for me Daddy."

She thumbed her hood all the way back, exposing her clitoris, "Please daddy, right here." She whimpered and pleaded like a spoiled child, begging him to bring his tongue to her.

She saw the debate in his mind on his face. He wanted to taste her, but something was stopping him. His tongue was rapidly running across his lips. She almost had him and she knew it. She opened her thighs wider and slid two fingers into herself. She put the pipe down, and worked on herself with both hands. She whined and she pleaded that she needed his tongue. She told him she didn't care if he killed her later just bring her his tongue now. She saw the debate end in his mind. He put the butcher knife by his side, and his head between her thighs.

****

He didn't use his tongue on the women he killed. He didn't give them that pleasure. He killed them, and that pleased him. But no woman had ever begged him like this one, and none had played with themselves the way she did. He would lick her, but he would kill her the moment he heard her have an orgasm. If she was moaning from playing with herself, he was certain she would scream when his tongue pushed her over the top. When he heard that scream, he would shove the knife into her body. His plan excited him. She would be the first woman he killed in the middle of a climax. He buried his head between her thighs.

****

Patrice did not hesitate. She locked her thighs around his head and squeezed. She grabbed the butcher knife with both her hands, taking it from his grip. He was clawing into her thighs and her back with the finger nails of his other hands. She ignored the pain and continued to

138

tighten her thighs. Her thighs were around his neck, and the butcher knife was in her hands. She crossed her ankles and squeezed with all her might. She brought the butcher knife down hard into the side of his face, into his jaw meat. She felt the knife go in. She pulled it out and brought it down again and again and again. He struggled and tried to get loose, but her thighs held him. The blade broke, but she continued to dig into his face and head with what was left of it.

When the only movement on the blanket was hers, she relaxed her thighs and rolled free. With hand trembling, she put her fingers on his bloody neck and checked for a pulse. There was none. She thanked God. She laid face down on the blanket, breathing heavily through her mouth.

The crazy bastard was dead.

Patrice tried twice to stand but fell. The pain ripped through her stomach and thighs. She crawled over to the cinder block wall, and eased herself up. She was weak but alive. She limped to the steps and stopped. She was naked. She had to have some type of clothing. She looked around the basement for her clothes. She saw them balled up in a plastic milk crate. She crept over to it, as if not to wake the dead crazy bastard. She slid on her white nurses aide uniform pants. She wasn't going to cry. She had to get out. Later when she told Samuel what happened, she would cry.

God, Samuel was waiting for her. She hadn't called him, hadn't told him a thing. He's going to know she'd been getting high. He's going to leave her for sure. Her feet hurt too much to put on her shoes or socks. She didn't want to stain her uniform blouse with blood, so she put on her coat without it. She checked her pants pocket for her paycheck money, it was there. Thank God.

Emotional Drippings

Samuel would believe her when she showed him the money. She had made up kidnapping stories before when she'd messed up money. The money would be the proof she needed. She hurried to the stairs. She tripped over the crazy bastard's kerosene lamp, and his duffle bag. The kerosene spilled and ran across the floor to the blanket. Her eyes followed the spilled liquid. If there was a fire, no one could tie her to the crazy bastard's death. She had not thought about going to the police. She was going home to Samuel and her kids. The crazy bastard was dead. Going to the police would only complicate her life. The kerosene was spreading towards the candles. There would be a fire.

She would tell Samuel the truth, that she'd been getting high for a couple of weeks, but that was all over now. God had given her another chance, and she was going to be honest from now on. Samuel would believe her. God wouldn't give her another chance if he was going to take Samuel and the kids away. Everything would work out fine.

When she tried to take the first step up her legs cramped in pain, the pain forced her to sit on the steps. She noticed several candles were flickering inches away from the kerosene and the corpse. She thought was, what if the kerosene didn't make to the candles. Her blood was all over the crazy bastard, and her fingerprints were everywhere. The police would find her. If she went to them, they would notify the state and her children would be taken again. No, she couldn't be tied to his death.

She rifled through his duffle bag looking for more kerosene. She found snapshot pictures of slain women. They had laid on the same blanket she had laid on. Some were taped and gagged as she had been. He had shoved the knife and candles into intimate parts of all the women. She counted nine murdered women.

She couldn't stop the tears.

God had truly spared her, maybe if she gave these pictures to the police. No. She was still involved, and they would still notify the state. She emptied the contents of the duffle bag on the floor: duct tape, ropes, clothes, a straight razor, carving knives, acid, lighter fluid, money, but no kerosene. She picked up the roll of money and dropped it in her coat pocket. She grabbed the duct tape, the pictures, and the lighter fluid. She limped over to his body and rolled him over. She taped the pictures to his chest and rolled him back over, face down. She squeezed out the remains of the lighter fluid on the blanket, and kicked a candle to the kerosene. She ran up the stairs and out the backdoor as best she could. She had left her shoes, her bra, her socks, and her uniform top. But she didn't go back for them. God's will be done.

The End

Emotional Drippings

The Last Time

I said I wasn't coming back over here. It doesn't make any sense for a man with my responsibilities to be out here doing the things I am doing. I have been married for ten years to a good woman. A woman whose heart would break if she found out what I been doing. I been out here bad like this for two months. Damn near every day, I been over here getting high and sticking my dick in a stripper.

I met her at my brother's bachelor party. She was one of eight strippers and wasn't nobody paying her any attention because she was so skinny. I like skinny women, always have, my wife is skinny. I like to pick a woman up and carry her around the room while fucking her.

At the bachelor party, my brother and his friends said she looked like a crack-head. They were right. She is a crack-head, and now she got me smoking that shit too. Yesterday when I was over here I told myself I wasn't never coming back because I spent three hundred dollars, but she fucked me good, and sucked my dick until I came out of my eyeballs, and then she swallowed the cum, and that freaky shit got me hard again right quick.

She texted me on my way home from work today and tempted me over with some asshole. A while ago I had told her I had never fucked a woman in the butt, and she said she would let me do it on a special day. She text me that today is that special day. So I drove over after work, and I am sitting in front of her court way building thinking hard about taking my stupid ass home.

Smoking crack ain't smart, anytime I do it every dime in my pocket gets spent. I got credit from her dope man last week and had to pay him back a hundred dollars on payday. I can't afford that shit. Today I got seventy-five dollars in my pocket, my cash for the week that covers lunches. I ain't ate lunch sense I been coming over here, all my pocket cash been going on crack. If I go in her place today that will lead to a tomorrow; and yesterday was to be my last time fucking with her and crack.

I shouldna answered her damn call, despite the text. I hadn't answered her calls, and she called me ten times. But she sent me a text when I got off work, talking about today was the special day. Then she typed in BOOTYHOLE in all caps. So here I am, parked in front of her building looking at about five droopy pants thugs hanging out in front of her door, two have been up in her place selling us crack. I really don't want to get out of my Subaru and walk through their crowd in my Dockers and pink button down shirt.

I work hard on trying not to look like I was born around the corner. Which I was, but when I got married I moved out of the 'hood. And my wife makes sure I don't dress like a person who has ever lived in the 'hood.

I really don't know these young cats, and would know nothing about them if she wouldna got me smoking crack. I live in the suburbs and work downtown. I ain't been in the 'hood in ten years. I pass by on the highway and don't even look in this direction. At least I didn't until I started cheating on my wife with this crack-head stripper.

I cut off the air and the engine. Flip, the guy I paid a hundred dollars to on payday is one of the five dudes in front of her building door. He sees me and nods his braided head towards me and begins making it over to my car. I roll the windows down and pop the locks. He gets in the front seat.

"What's up, Ben? You goin' up to Wendy?"

He smells sweaty and like weed.

Emotional Drippings

"Thinking about it, dude."

"She been waiting for you. She told me earlier you was coming through."

I look at him and see half a grin on his face. His top two teeth are showing, one is chipped at the bottom, and the other is capped in silver. His lip is covering his bottom teeth. Flip and I are both, what my wife calls, pecan brown.

He leans toward me and says, "Hey I want to tell you this here. I usually don't be in her business, her being my older sister and all because she don't like me pryin'. . ."

I interrupt him with, "Your sister?" My guess is that Flip is about twenty or twenty-one. I never asked Wendy how old she was. Guessing, I'd say late twenties early thirties around my age.

"Yeah, you didn't know that? What you thought just anybody would give her a hundred dollar credit play? Not. Especially not around here. But look here. This is what I want you to know. She ain't gonna tell you this here, but since she been fucking around with you, she ain't been stripping or out here getting her hustle on.

"Matter of fact, she don't get high unless she with you. What I'm saying man is that you slowing her down on all that bullshit. Lately she been talking about finding a job and shit. My sister ain't said nothing like that in three years. She used to go to work every day. But her old nigga turned her out on rocks, and you know the story. I just wanted to let you know you doin' somethin' for her."

He is nodding his head in the affirmative while looking me in my eyes. He is looking at me like my father used to do when he was checking to make sure I was listening.

I nod my head in the affirmative and say, "I hear you man."

With the air conditioner off the car has gotten hot and muggy even with the windows down. I reach into my pocket and peel off fifty dollars and hand it to him. He reaches into his socks pulls out a little clear plastic baggy. He picks out six ten dollar bags of rocks and hands them to me.

"Y'all have fun up there." He opens the door and gets out the car.

I roll up my windows, get out, and hit the key pad locking my car. I follow Flip to the building and through the group of young men. He remains with the group of thugs, and I walk through the building doors. Walking up the creaky, dirty, red, carpeted stairs I think about what he said. I have made a difference in Wendy's life.

I hadn't thought much about her life. Yeah she had told me stuff, but I wasn't listening. I was either sucking on the crack pipe or getting my dick sucked. We weren't in a relationship. I was just tricking off, and she was a stripper with good head. She did tell me that after her baby son died her old man started getting high and she did too. I heard her, but I really didn't. She had lost a child, and I only thought about it while she was saying it.

When she opens the recently painted brown door, I really look at her. I see a slim black woman with a short afro, pretty eyes, thick lips, and smile that could melt an iceberg. I am glad I came over. Seeing her always excites me physically. I like how this woman looks.

"Oh," she says with her small head bobbing for emphasis, "So, a bitch got to say you getting some asshole to get you over here, huh?" She asks with sly smirk on her face.

I pull her into my arms, hug her, and kiss her lips. We are in an embrace and I'm looking into pretty round eyes. I say, "You ain't a bitch."

Emotional Drippings

"Whatever, nigga," is her reply.

She is smiling now, not smirking, and she hasn't pulled from my embrace, so I kiss her again. This time she opens her mouth and our tongues go into each other's mouth. I pick her up and kick her door closed behind me. She wraps her legs around my back and her duster comes open. She is naked under the pale gray duster. She knows I like to do it carrying her, and she is positioning herself to allow me inside her. I open my belt and my Dockers fall around my oxblood penny loafers. I pop my hard dick free of my briefs and go right into her.

"You ass be wanting me bad. You can't even come in my place without being hard."

She settles down on my dick and I am completely inside her. I attempt a step, but I have to kick my Dockers free of my ankles to walk and fuck. My pants take flight when I kick them free, and they land across the small studio apartment on top of a suitcase by the twelve inch color television set.

When I get to her daybed we lower to it and go at it. I enjoy fucking her as much as I do my wife. Both of their pussies have a glove fit. Wendy's is a bit more shallow, allowing me to reach her tender spot in any position. She has wrapped her legs around my back giving me all of her, so I go deep and stay deep, and cum faster than I wanted to. She massages my dick with her pussy walls draining all I have. I lie still for moments.

"You must of drove all the way from downtown thinking about fucking me?"

"Yes, I did."

"And does it feels like you want it to feel?"

"Yes, it does."

Again she tightens her pussy walls around my dick, massaging me while I am inside her. My wife doesn't do this. This is Wendy trick, one that gets me hard right after I cum. I can get hard a second time with Wendy easily because she is always doing something to excite me; either saying some freaky shit or doing some freaky shit like licking my balls or pulling on my nipples. I never know what to expect from her and that excites me. And that leads to us doing again right away.

I roll off and out of her because if I cum back to back the chances of me getting hard again are slim, especially after I smoke some crack. And I want to get hard again because of the special treat she has promised. The crack rocks are still in my hand. I pass them to her.

"You must of saw Flip down stairs?"

"Yep, and he gave me six for fifty."

"He better had. As much money as you spend with his ass."

She takes off her duster, and I take off my shirt and t-shirt and throw them to the foot of the daybed. She reaches beneath the daybed and brings up a glass cylinder pipe, a plate, and a lighter. She opens up one of the small bags with her teeth and puts half of a rock on the glass pipe and lights it. I slide down and get between her thighs. If I give her head while she's smoking she gets real freaky, and today I want her real freaky.

I keep my tongue flicking around and on her clit because I don't want any of my own sperm in my mouth. She likes me to stay on her clit anyway.

"Damn, Ben," she moans, "You know how I like it."

And I do, pleasing her came natural to me. She likes to have done to her what I like to do. When I feel her body quiver, and see the pipe and lighter roll from her hand to the side of the daybed I know she is

147

Emotional Drippings

cumming.

I rise up from between her thighs and join her on the pillow.

She opens her eyes and looks at me and says, "When you didn't answer my calls I thought you was tired of me. You know everything ends, and I thought we had ended. But your body tells me different, you ain't tired of me. You still want me."

"Is that a question?"

"Naw, nigga. That's a fact, you ass just as sprung on me as I am on you."

"You sprung on me?" I ask looking at her full lips,

"Every since the bachelor party, you make me feel special, Ben, and that's why I am going to do something special for you and me today."

She winks, and I am getting hard in expectation. My brother talks about fucking an asshole like it is the best thing a person can do during sex.

"I douched it out nice and clean for you. This is not something I do all the time, so it's real tight. You gonna have to wait on taking a hit of rock because you have to be real hard to get inside a bootyhole. And you can't be frantic. It has to be done nice and easy. Understand?"

She has a serious expression on her slender face. I tell her, "Yeah, I understand."

"I had to go up to drug store and by some lubricant because I don't be doing this." She says continuing to look at me sternly. As if she wants me to say, 'that's ok we don't have to do it.' But I am not going say that. I want to do it, and am all the hard in anticipation.

"Reach under the bed and get that tube of stuff." She half heartedly says.

I get the tube.

"Now squeeze some out on your finger, a lot and just one finger to start."

Once I get a big glob on my finger she directs my hand down to her bootyhole, "Now rub it up in there until your finger slides in and out smoothly.

She is right, her bootyhole is tight. I am barely able to get my lubed finger in. Once I have worked all the glob in, I squirt another glob on my finger and repeat the process. My finger is sliding in and out easily.

"Now oil up two fingers, and do until the two fingers go in and out smoothly."

I doesn't seems like I am going to get the two fingers in without hurting her so I squirt out a lot of the lubricant some directly on her bootyhole opening and more on my fingers. Eventually both fingers are going in and out easily.

"Ok," she says, "let's do this. And remember, slow and easy." She pulls her knees back and spreads her thighs.

I put my dick on her greased opening and push. I'm in and damn it's tight. It feels like I can push in some more, so I do, and more, and more.

"Hold it! That's enough for now, move it back and forth right there."

It feels sorta like a pussy just tighter around the opening. And it's so slippery inside that I really can't feel her side walls like in her pussy. I push in deeper and she exhales.

"Ok, put it all in."

And I do, and damn it does feel good. She is clamping down on my dick every time I back it out, and the grip is way tighter than her pussy,

Emotional Drippings

but she only grips when I'm pulling it out not going in.

"Put it all in and don't move."

I do it, and she is squeezing my dick. If I wanted to pull it out I couldn't, that's how firm the grip is. I have no choice but to cum and collapse on top of her. She is squeezing my dick so tight that it feels like she is milking the sperm out of it while it is inside her bootyhole.

"Damn," is all I can say in response to her pulsating grips.

"Pull it out while I'm holding you tight like this," she directs.

"I can't, you holding it too tight."

"Pull it back."

I try again and she eases up on the grip a bit, but once I pull some out again she tightens. I pull more out, and she fist tightens around my dick head, making me cum again.

Out of her, I roll off of her.

I look down at my dick and it has never been that long; soft or hard. She stretched my dick, and it has some bobo on the tip. I want to stand up and go wash my dick, but I don't have the energy to move. Wendy gets up out of the day bed and goes into the bathroom. I hear the water running. She comes back with toilet paper, a soapy rag and a rinse rag. She cleans me off and I say, "thanks baby." But I know I still need to go in that bathroom and wash my own dick. My brother didn't tell me anything about getting bobo on my dick.

I grab the pipe, a bag and the lighter from the plate on the floor. I put the whole bag on the glass pipe and light it.

While I am exhaling Wendy asks, "Did you like what we did?"

I lay back on the pillow and say, "Ain't never did nothing like it before, but honestly . . . I like the pussy better, much better." And that's the truth, pussy feels better and there is no shit on your dick after. I light the pipe again and blow out a big cloud of smoke. She scoots up next to me but sits by my head and doesn't lie down.

"Do you think that today will be a special memory for you? Will you remember it? " She asks looking down at me.

"Yeah I'ma remember it. I ain't saying I never want to do it again, I'm just saying the pussy is better."

She bends to me and kisses me on the lips and says, "That's because you a man, not a gay booty-hole-buster, but I did it so you won't have to be all curious about it. Now you know all about it." She kisses me again.

Sitting back up she says, "Ben, it's something I have to tell you and I hope you won't be upset about it."

I hand her the pipe.

"No not right now. I got to tell this first."

I light the pipe again. "Tell me," I exhale.

"I need you to drive me out to the drug rehab. They got a bed for me. It's a ninety day inpatient treatment center. I been trying to get in for a month. I tried to tell you yesterday that they called me, but we was into getting high, and I didn't get to tell you."

I just took three hits so I am high, and I am sexually spent, and now she wants to talk serious. But I did hear her, so I sit up straight and say, "Ninety days, damn that's three months."

"I know, but when I'm finished they help me relocate and find a job."

"Relocate?"

"Yeah, the program is successful because people really get a new start through it. I am going to Denver."

"They got crack in Denver."

Emotional Drippings

"Yeah, but I will have to find it. It won't be at my door waiting for me to come outside. Will you drive me out to the center, it's in the 'burbs?"

I wipe my hand over my face trying to clear my mind and say, "You serious."

"As a heart attack," she answers.

"What about your place?"

"I'm leaving it. My brother can have the television and this daybed if he wants them. Everything I else I own is in that suitcase."

She nods her head to where I kicked my Dockers.

"I told you, today was special for me and you. I tried to tell you yesterday but we didn't talk, only smoked."

I ran my hand across her thighs, "So you breaking up with me?"

It should be kind of a funny thought, since I was going to end it with her, but for some reason the shit don't feel funny at all.

"No," she reaches over and grips my thigh, "don't look at it like that. I am doing something for me, trying to get my real life back. You got a wife, and a job, and a car. You got a life. I want to get where you are. But I won't get there sitting up in here smoking crack. Now, will you give me a ride out there?"

I don't know if being married, working, and having a car note equals life. But I understand what she's saying. And if she wouldn't have just gave me some pussy and some asshole I wouldn't be tripping at all. So I say, "Hell yeah, I will give you a ride, girl. Shit, that ain't no problem."

I try again to pass her the pipe.

"Nope, you can finish those off. I'm tired of that shit . . . really, I am."

I look at the remaining bags of crack on the plate, the pipe in my hand, and then to Wendy's hopeful face. I see that she is really happy about leaving then I think about my wife, my job, and my life. I think about the stripper that I blamed for starting me smoking crack.

Wendy is more than that. She is a woman taking a chance on a new life. And if I pick up one of those rocks, it's me wanting to smoke not Wendy getting me to smoke. I drop the pipe, and tell her, "Let's ride."

It didn't take her five minutes to get dressed, and it didn't take me five minutes to shower and really wash my dick.

In the car she tells me, "Denver ain't that far, and if a man really wanted to see a woman he could."

I start the Subaru and think about how good she had me feeling upstairs, and I think about what was supposed to be our last time and realize that, "One never knows. Life is full of surprises."

"Whatever, nigga," is her smiling reply.

The End